WIZARD IN WONDERLAND

Books by the same author:

After Thursday
Hi There, Supermouse!
If It Weren't For Sebastian
One Green Leaf
The Other Side of the Fence
Plague
See You Thursday
What If They Saw Me Now?
The Wizard in the Woods
You Win Some, You Lose Some

WIZARD
IN
WONDERLAND

by Jean Ure
Illustrated by
David Anstey

CANDLEWICK PRESS
CAMBRIDGE, MASSACHUSETTS

First U.S. edition 1993
First published in Great Britain in 1991 by
Walker Books Ltd., London.

Library of Congress Cataloging-in-Publication Data:

Ure, Jean   Wizard in Wonderland/Jean Ure;
illustrated by David Anstey. — 1st U.S. edn.
Summary: Joel and Gemma are enjoying a visit to Wonderland
with their friend, junior wizard Ben-Muzzy, when his
magic broomstick is stolen by the Airy Fairies.
[1. Fantasy.]
I. Anstey, David, ill.   II. Title.
PZ7.U64Wk   1993   [Fic]—dc20   92-53020
ISBN 1-56402-138-6

10 9 8 7 6 5 4 3 2 1

Printed in the U.S.A.

Candlewick Press
2067 Massachusetts Avenue
Cambridge, Massachusetts 02140

For Sophie
when she is old enough

Chapter One

The twins were in the sitting room watching television when the broomstick came down the chimney. It arrived with a great whooshing and swooshing, nimbly avoided a big vase of dried flowers standing in the hearth, and shot quivering to a halt in the fireplace.

"Wow!" said Joel.

"That was neat," said Gemma.

It was just as well the twins were by themselves. If their mother had been there, she might have been alarmed at the sight of a broomstick appearing in her living room. She might even have telephoned the police and complained about people dropping dangerous objects out of the sky.

The twins weren't alarmed, once they saw what it was. How else, after all, would you expect a broomstick to arrive, if not down a chimney?

The broomstick, with a businesslike air, propped itself against the mantelpiece.

"Look!" cried Joel. "It's got a label!"

"It must be a message from Ben-Muzzy!"

The twins scrambled eagerly over the back of the sofa, followed closely by Primple, a small, shaggy dog with a pink nose and a curly tail.

(How many times had their mother told them, "*Don't jump around on the furniture*"? But it wasn't every day you received messages from a wizard.)

The label had obviously been tied with a special magic knot. Not even Gemma, who was cat's cradle champion of the fourth grade could find a way of unscrambling it.

"Oh, don't bother!" Joel, impatient as usual, elbowed his twin out of the way. "Let's see what it says."

On one side, in green capital letters, were the words:

RETURN TO SENDER

and in smaller letters underneath:

PROPERTY OF WOLLIBAR G.H.W.

Wollibar was the wizard Ben-Muzzy worked for. Ben-Muzzy was only a junior wizard, but Wollibar was a full Grand High and was entitled to put letters after his name.

The other side of the label, in a small spidery hand, read:

I am on holly day. Meet me in the wood, same as before for FUN AND ADVENCHER. One hour from now.
PS Rite yes if you can and no if you cant.
B. Muzzy

"*Advencher?*" scoffed Joel. "*Holly* day? Don't they teach wizards how to spell?"

"Probably not," said Gemma. "I guess they

have more important things to learn, like how to fly broomsticks and do magic spells."

"Yes, we all know about Ben-Muzzy's spells," said Joel.

Ben-Muzzy's spells were like Gemma's math problems: They had a tendency to end up wrong. Primple was one of Ben-Muzzy's spells that had gone wrong. He had long shaggy hair and short stubby legs, one ear that stuck up and one ear that hung down, and a scrubbing-brush fringe that sprouted absurdly from the top of his head.

"I hope Wollibar knows that Ben-Muzzy's taken his broomstick." Joel looked around for a pen to write their reply. "There'll be trouble if he doesn't."

"I don't see why," said Gemma. "After all, it was Ben-Muzzy who found it."

"Actually, we *all* found it."

"Actually, we stole it."

"Only from a bunch of moldy old witches."

"Well, anyway," said Gemma, "it was Ben-Muzzy who flew it back. And Wollibar *said* he could use it to come visiting."

"Just as long as he asked," said Joel with an

air of self-righteousness. "After what happened before, I would think he'd try to avoid trouble for a while."

What had happened before was that quite by accident, in the middle of a spell, Ben-Muzzy made himself disappear. All the Grand High Wizards in the land had to get together and try to find him again. They were all extremely angry, what with having to magic themselves long distances and interrupt work on any number of important spells. "Total carelessness!" had snapped Wollibar.

"As long as he got permission," said Joel, "that's all." Standing on one leg, he balanced the label on his knees. YES, he wrote.

Ben-Muzzy may or may not have gotten Wollibar's permission, but Joel wasn't missing out on an opportunity for fun.

"There!" He twitched the label back into place around the broomstick's handle. "Now what do we do?"

As if in answer to his question, the broomstick slowly leaned away from the mantelpiece, tilted itself lengthwise, floated into the middle of the room, took careful aim at the chimney, and in

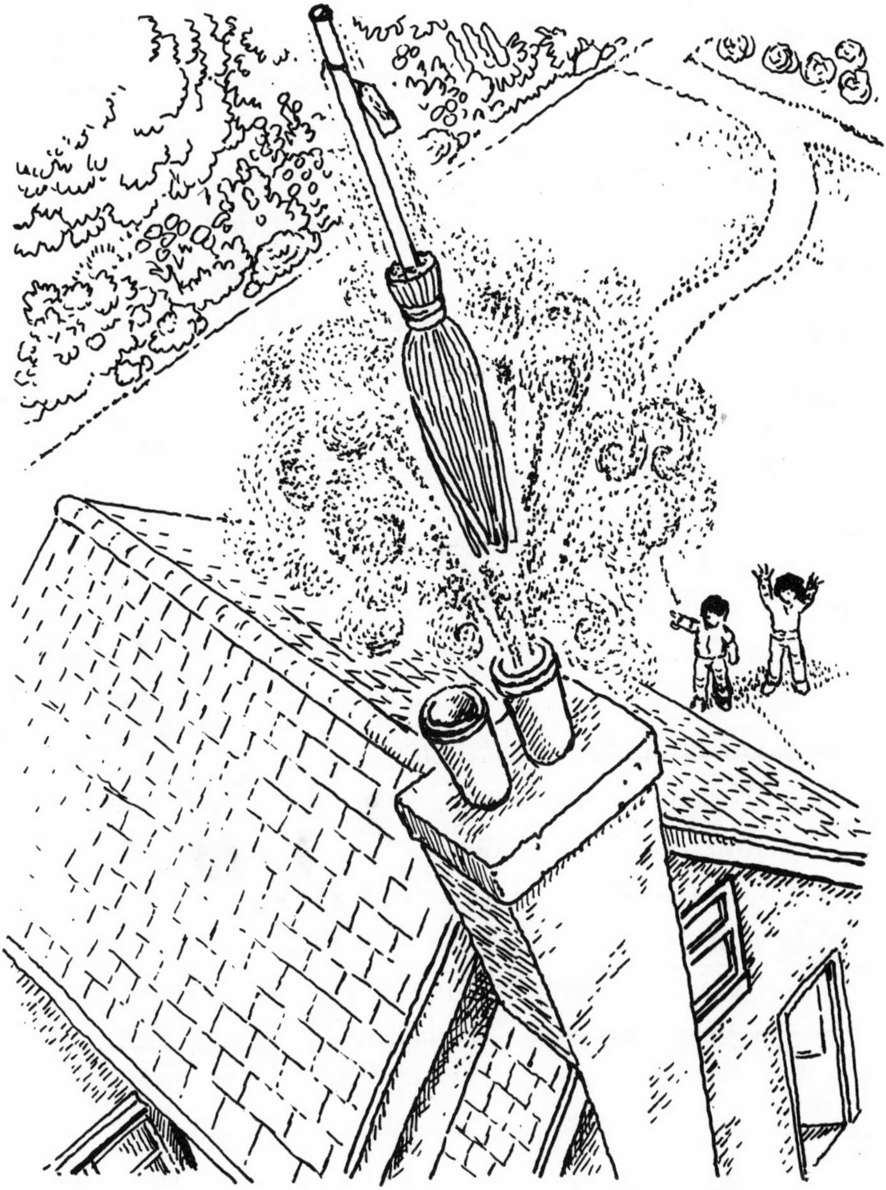

one quick *zoomf!* disappeared.

"Let's go and watch it come out!" yelled Joel. They zoomed into the garden through the french windows, just in time to see the broomstick shoot out of the chimney and go hurtling like a rocket into space.

"That is some piece of flying," said Joel. "Just wait till I tell Graham Roberts!"

"Never mind telling Graham Roberts," said Gemma. "What are we going to tell Mom?" They could hardly tell her they were going to go adventuring with a wizard.

"We'll just say we're going to the woods," decided Joel.

After all, they *were* going to the woods. They might even *stay* in the woods.

"Not if he's coming by broomstick," said Gemma, reading her twin's thoughts as she often did. "You can go anywhere you want by broomstick."

"Well, I'm certainly not going anywhere by Ben-Muzzy's magic," said Joel. "Not after last time."

"N-no . . ." Even Gemma had to admit that last time had been almost *too* adventurous. Ben-

Muzzy had been captured by an ogre, Joel had been turned into a puddle of mud, and they had all three had a narrow escape when a raven had gotten into the magic circle and ruined the spell and they had landed slap-bang in the middle of a Grand Meeting of Witches.

"I wouldn't mind a *little* adventure," said Gemma, "but only as long as we can get out of it as soon as we've had enough."

"But we should take provisions," urged Joel. "Just in case."

The twins' mother was used to them going off to the woods. She packed their knapsacks with apples and sandwiches, and chocolate cake and bottles of orange juice and told them to have a good time. She thought they were going to play marbles and make dens in the bracken. She had no idea they were going to go adventuring with a wizard.

"Be back for dinner," she said. That was exactly what she had said last time.

"And we did get back," said Gemma, "so it was perfectly all right."

They found Ben-Muzzy waiting for them in

exactly the same spot where they had found him
before.

When they had found him before he was
sitting at the foot of a tree, weeping because he'd
made himself disappear and didn't know where
he was. Today he was standing there in his green
cloak and his red pointed shoes, with one arm

hooked around the broomstick, for all the world as if he had been flying broomsticks since he was in his cradle.

"Oh, good!" cried Gemma. "You've brought it!"

"Hope you've learned to fly it better than last time," said Joel. "I seem to remember that we *almost* didn't get away from those witches on account of you not knowing how to start it properly. Why are you on vacation, anyway? We don't have vacation for another two weeks."

Ben-Muzzy explained, "It's National Cauldron Day. No one does any magic on National Cauldron Day, except if it's an emergency. It's to give the cauldrons a rest. So I thought I'd come and get you, and we'd all go to Wonderland and go up the Dream Ladder."

"That sounds fun!" said Gemma, at exactly the same moment as Joel said, "What's a dream ladder?"

"Climb the Dream Ladder ... make your dreams come true!"

Joel looked at Ben-Muzzy suspiciously. "How's it do that?"

"I don't know *how* it does it," said Ben-

Muzzy. "But it does it . . . Podnock went up it last year." (Podnock was Wollibar's other assistant.) "He dreamt he'd invented this special, brand-new spell that no one had ever invented before, and he was invited to a garden party to meet the Wizard of all Wizards and was given an honor in the New Moon's honors list."

"What was the spell?" said Gemma. "The one that he invented?"

"Unfortunately," said Ben-Muzzy, "he forgot it as soon as he came down."

"Ha!" said Joel.

Gemma kicked him.

"Well, but that's not making your dreams come true," grumbled Joel. "Not if you're just going to go and forget them again."

"He didn't forget it *all*," said Gemma.

"Podnock said it was just like real," said Ben-Muzzy. "He wanted to go back this year and do it again, but then he let the cauldron boil over and Wollibar said he had to spend the day cleaning it instead. So I thought *we'd* go," said Ben-Muzzy. "Without him."

"I s'pose you want to dream the same sort of thing," said Joel slyly. "See if you can get to meet the Big Shot Wizard geezer."

Ben-Muzzy blushed. (It was true that the thought had occurred to him.)

"Can you dream whatever you want?" said Gemma.

"Absolutely anything."

"I know what I'm going to dream!" Gemma clapped her hands excitedly. "I'm going to dr——"

"Hang on!" cried Joel. There were times when Gemma got a little too carried away. "Where *is* this place, exactly?"

"Not far. Just a short broomstick ride."

"And what is it, exactly?"

Ben-Muzzy's eyes gleamed in his pointy wizard's face. "It's where people go to have fun!"

"Like a fun-fair?" said Gemma. "Does it have slot machines and cotton candy and games you can play? And bumper cars and fortune tellers and funny hats? And merry-go-rounds and roller coasters and —"

"Everything," said Ben-Muzzy.

"Then let's go!" Gemma did one of her little twirls. (She was always doing twirls. It kind of embarrassed Joel.) "What are we waiting for?"

Ben-Muzzy moved away from the broomstick, which remained standing upright by itself.

"I'll just get her started," said Ben-Muzzy. Casually he waved a hand. "*Esir!*" he said. The broomstick rose obligingly into the air. "*Pots!*" The broomstick stopped. "*Esrever!*"

Slowly the broomstick reversed and lowered itself until it was within a few feet of the ground.

"I'm impressed!" said Gemma.

"Oh, it's nothing," said Ben-Muzzy airily. "Not to a wizard."

He must have been practicing, thought Joel jealously. He hadn't been able to do that the last time they traveled by broomstick. But then there wasn't anything much to *starting*. Even Joel knew how to start the family car, (not that he was allowed to).

"I suppose —" Joel said it carelessly —"I suppose Wollibar does know you've got the broomstick?"

Ben-Muzzy gave a little hum and pretended he hadn't heard. With the corner of his cloak he flicked at a speck of dust.

"Well?" said Joel. "Does he or doesn't he?"

Ben-Muzzy looked a little sulky. "Wollibar's gone off to a special cauldron conference. We'll

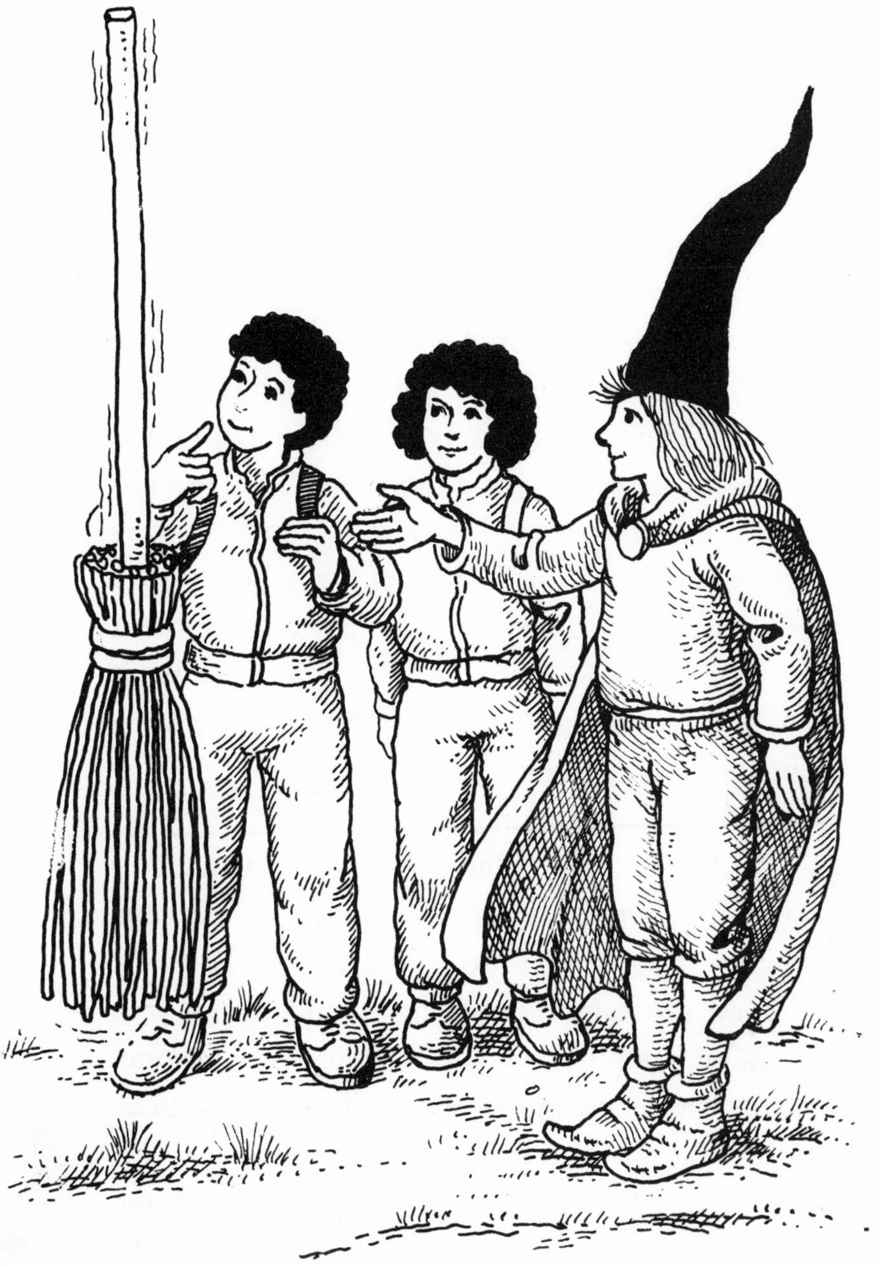

be back ages before he is."

"You mean you *haven't* asked him? Well! You'll be in trouble if anything goes wrong."

"What can go wrong," said Gemma, "with a broomstick?"

Ben-Muzzy muttered, "Nothing."

The truth was, he felt guilty. He should have asked Wollibar. The only reason he hadn't was that the last time he'd borrowed the broomstick — *with* permission, just to practice — he crash-landed in the middle of a senior wizard's cauldron and ruined a very important spell that was brewing. Wollibar had said sternly that if Ben-Muzzy couldn't be trusted to fly a broomstick with due care and attention, then he had better not fly one at all.

Joel was right. There would be trouble if anything went wrong. Wollibar was already angry enough as it was, what with Podnock letting the cauldron boil over and Ben-Muzzy ruining people's spells. But then, as Gemma said, what *could* go wrong? With a broomstick?

Ben-Muzzy immediately felt cheerful again. Hadn't he flown them all safely back from the Land of the Witches? Why, he'd had more experience with broomsticks than some wizards twice his age!

"All aboard!" sang Ben-Muzzy. "Take your seats, ladies and gentlemen, please!"

Gemma climbed onto the broomstick behind Ben-Muzzy. Joel settled himself behind Gemma.

"All present and correct?" said Ben-Muzzy. "Ready for takeoff? OK, then . . . *Og stel!*"

The broomstick tipped its nose into the air, rose uncertainly, hovered a moment, then hit the earth again with a jolt.

"Ow," said Gemma.

"It looks like we've stalled," said Joel.

Gemma could see, in the gap between Ben-Muzzy's hat and the top of his cloak, that his neck had turned bright red.

"I guess," she said kindly, "that it didn't hear you."

Joel sniggered. "More likely we've run out of gas."

"Stupid," said Gemma. "Broomsticks don't need *gas*."

"So what is it, then? What's he done?"

"Don't panic," said Ben-Muzzy, recovering himself. "I just forgot to tell it where we're going. What I should have said —"

What he should have said was, "Let's go to Wonderland," which in broomstick talk was — was —

"What's he up to *now?*" hissed Joel.

"Sh!" said Gemma. "He's trying to figure it all out."

"Work what out? I thought he was supposed to be an expert? I th——"

"*Quiet,*" said Gemma. "It's not easy, talking backward to a broomstick. A person needs to concentrate."

Ben-Muzzy concentrated. He tipped his hat back and wiped a hand across his forehead. This was terrible! He had forgotten how to say "Wonderland" backward! Dna . . . Dna . . .

"*Dnalrednow!*" shouted Ben-Muzzy triumphantly.

They were off!

Chapter Two

"Wheeeee!" caroled Ben-Muzzy, diving down an air current and plunging headfirst into a cloud bank. "Get out of my way!" roared Ben-Muzzy, scattering a flock of startled pigeons. "Road hogs!" he bellowed.

It had to be said that Ben-Muzzy was not the safest of broomstick fliers.

"It should have license plates," grumbled Joel, clinging on for dear life as the sky whirled dizzily around them.

"Blurp!" went Gemma's stomach. She wondered if she was going to be sick.

"Hurrooo!" bawled Ben-Muzzy, lifting both hands in the air.

The next second there was a bone-shattering

jolt as the broomstick plummeted earthward.

"*Oh!*" gasped Gemma.

"License plates!" yelled Joel.

Ben-Muzzy's hands hastily clamped back again. (Wollibar would be furious if he went and crash-landed a second time.)

"What happened?" quavered Gemma, as the broomstick slowly righted itself.

"Unexpected current. Happens all the time. No need to worry. We broomstickers —" Ben-Muzzy waved a hand and the broomstick veered sharply to one side. Gemma's stomach lurched — "We broomstickers are used to that sort of thing."

Showing off, thought Joel sourly.

"I hope we're almost there," said Gemma. "'Cause if we're n-not —" If they weren't, she thought she was going to have to get off and be sick.

"Land ahoy!" shouted Ben-Muzzy.

Gemma risked a quick peep over the side. Far below she could see throngs of colorfully dressed people milling to and fro, and clusters of buildings, dazzling white like iced cakes in the sunshine.

"*Og ew nwod!*" chanted
Ben-Muzzy, in control
once more.

On their way down,
they passed through a
mass of what Gemma at
first took to be petals
floating in the air. A
second glance showed
her that they weren't
petals but tiny creatures,
with shimmering silver
bodies and tissue-paper
wings in delicate shades
of pink and purple, of
lemon and lilac and
palest blue, like a garden
full of sweet peas.

"Oh! Oh! Stop!" pleaded
Gemma, reaching out a hand
in a vain attempt to catch one.
All the little creatures squeaked
and shrilled, floating just out
of reach. "Oh, do be careful!"
she begged. "You nearly ran

one down!"

"It's their own fault," said Ben-Muzzy. "If they get in the way when a broomstick's coming in to land —"

"Oh, but the poor little *things*," crooned Gemma, as petals went scattering in all directions. "You're frightening them!"

Ben-Muzzy hitched his cloak indifferently. "They're only Airy Fairies. They haven't got enough brains to be frightened. All they ever do is hang around making a nuisance of themselves. . . . They're too light to land unless it's absolutely calm. Even then they can only stay down for a few seconds. *No* brain, *no* body weight . . . totally useless."

"They must serve some purpose," objected Joel. (He had just been studying ecology in school.) "Everything serves *some* purpose."

Ben-Muzzy thought about it as the broomstick swept in a wide circle looking for a suitable place to land.

"They shine in the dark," he said. "But that's about all. Mostly they're just a stupid nuisance."

"Like girls," said Joel. He only said it to annoy Gemma. He liked to put her in her place now and again, especially as she usually beat him in class. But the broomstick had landed and already Gemma was climbing off.

"Oh, this is *terrific!* Absolutely terrific!" she said.

"I knew you'd like it," said Ben-Muzzy.

All around, as far as the eye could see, were stalls offering things to eat, things to drink, ornaments, trinkets, "Presents from Wonderland."

Hidden bands played music. People screamed on the Zig-Zag Rounder, whirled in space inside a Flying Helmet, diced with death on the Giant Spider. Even Joel admitted that it looked tempting. There was only one problem, he suddenly realized.

"We didn't bring any money!" he shouted despairingly above the hubbub. "How can we go on things if we don't have any money?"

"You don't need money," shouted back Ben-Muzzy. "Everything's free."

"Free?" Gemma's eyes widened. "Oh, even more terrific! Let's go and do things!"

They left the broomstick where it was, parked against a tree. Joel wanted to know whether it shouldn't be chained up, but Ben-Muzzy pooh-poohed the suggestion. Nobody stole things in a land where everything was free, and in any case, no one but a wizard could make a broomstick fly.

"Or a witch," Gemma reminded him.

Or a witch, agreed Ben-Muzzy. But witches weren't allowed in Wonderland. They had descended on it one year and almost wrecked the place. Now there was a ban on them.

"See?"

The twins looked and saw a large notice that said:

NO HAWKERS NO CIRCULARS
NO WITCHES by order

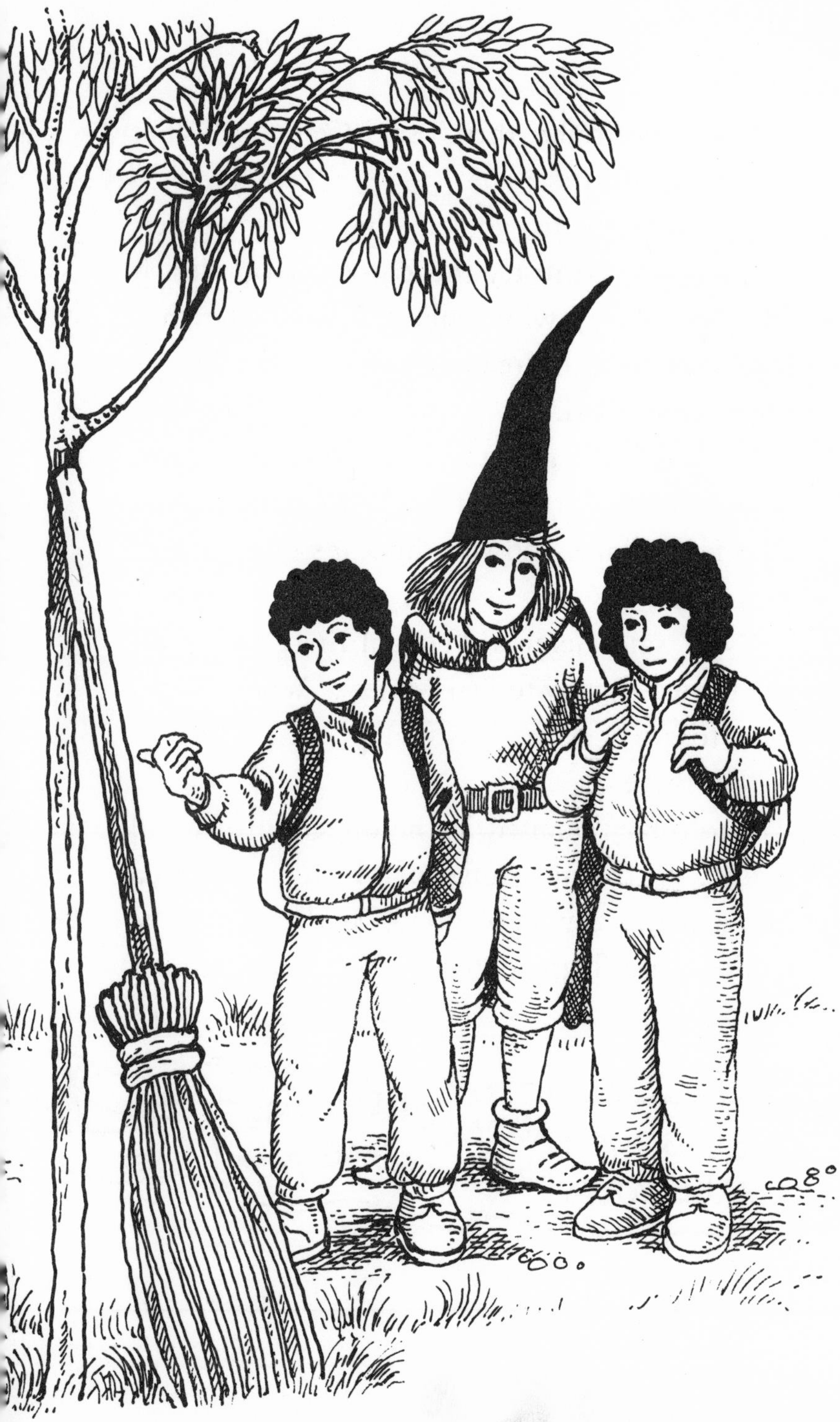

"That's all right, then," said Gemma. "What should we do first?"

Joel wanted to go on the Giant Spider, Gemma wanted to try the Zig-Zag Rounder. It was Ben-Muzzy who reminded them that they had come here to dream. "You can do all those things afterward."

Joel said, "We might not have time afterward. Not if we've got to get back for dinner. And talking of dinner, do you think it's time to start eating yet?"

"No," said Gemma. "Dream first, eat later." She turned eagerly to Ben-Muzzy. "Where do we have to go?"

"Up there."

Ben-Muzzy pointed in the direction of a tall ladder, the topmost rungs of which disappeared into a swirling mass of cloud. By the side of the ladder was a flagpole, from which flew a banner saying:

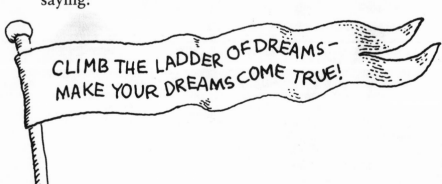

CLIMB THE LADDER OF DREAMS — MAKE YOUR DREAMS COME TRUE!

"I think dreaming's silly," said Joel.

Gemma tossed her head. "You can think what you like! It doesn't matter to me one little bit what you think. *I'm* going to go and dream, that's all I know."

Gemma and Ben-Muzzy set off toward the ladder. Joel followed, mumbling. Anyone would think that it was those two who were twins. They were even dressed alike — Gemma in her green track suit, Ben-Muzzy in his green cloak. Joel, in bright scarlet, felt like a sore thumb. Gemma *always* took Ben-Muzzy's side.

"Stop sulking," said Gemma, turning back to wait for him. "Look! There's a stall that has practical jokes . . . *Goofy Gags to Play on Your Friends*. You could get something to play on Graham Roberts . . . Festering Scab. You could get a festering scab and stick it on the back of his leg when he wasn't looking and say, 'Ugh, you've got a yucky festering scab!' *That* would frighten him."

Joel sniffed.

"Or what about Exploding Bubble Gum or Stinky Slime or —" Gemma's eye suddenly caught something —"Stickjaw Toffee! *Guaran-*

teed to stick jaws. That would keep him from talking in class. Why not get some of that?"

"You get it," said Joel, trying to pretend to himself that he was above such childish pranks. (In fact he rather liked the idea of sticking Graham Roberts's jaws together. It would pay Graham Roberts back for the time he put a plastic maggot in Joel's dinner.)

"All right." Gemma snatched a packet of toffee as she passed. It felt almost like stealing, but it was what everyone else was doing.

There was a line of people waiting to go up the ladder. Gemma, who could never stand still for more than a few seconds, whiled away the time by hopping up and down and chanting, "I know what *I'm* going to dream! I know what *I'm* going to dream!" Joel wished she wouldn't do it. It was so embarrassing. People were looking at her and smiling. He was sure Mom and Dad wouldn't approve.

At last they set foot on the ladder. Gemma, despite being scared of heights, was up as fast as anyone. She couldn't wait to start dreaming.

I don't know about this, thought Joel. I really

don't know about this.

They had climbed only a few feet when they found themselves with their heads in the clouds.

"Ooo! Look!" squealed Gemma. She turned and reached for Joel. "There's the Queen of England!"

Joel looked. A few rungs above them was a big, fat woman with a large bottom. She wore a bright yellow bathing suit with orange spots and had a frilly bathing cap on her head. She didn't bear even the slightest resemblance to the Queen.

"I've seen the Queen!" breathed Gemma reverently. "Wearing her crown!"

On the rung above Gemma, Ben-Muzzy was solemnly bowing, leaning out from the ladder in order to do so. Had *he* seen the Queen as well?

He turned, put a hand to his mouth, and hissed, "The Wizard of all Wizards . . . here! In Wonderland!"

"Where?" said Joel.

"Oh, he's gone now," said Ben-Muzzy. "He was only passing."

Crazy, thought Joel. Both of them were absolutely, positively crazy.

After a few more rungs they came to a platform. Ben-Muzzy explained that you could either stay on this level and browse, or you could move on to more exalted levels and start dreaming in earnest. Both Gemma and Ben-Muzzy, needless to say, were in favor of moving on.

"I'll stay here," said Joel. "You can pick me up when you're finished."

He moved across to the edge of the platform, peering out through the clouds. Suddenly, as he was peering, a face bobbed up beside him, looming at him out of the mist. It gave him quite a shock. It was a large, mournful face with floppy ears and droopy whiskers. Its eyes were baggy and its nose and mouth seemed not quite certain where they should be in relation to each other. If it looked like anything at all, which on the whole it didn't, it looked like a hand-knitted shopping bag full of oatmeal.

"Hilloo!" said the shopping bag, in a soft, bleaty voice. "Does I know you?"

Joel swallowed. Take no notice, he thought, and it will go away.

"Got any grub?" said the shopping bag,

hanging its head over the side of the platform. It nuzzled hopefully at Joel's pocket.

This is beyond a joke, thought Joel. "Only peppermints," he said.

"Peppermints is OK. Wallopers isn't fussy. Wallopers eats all grub."

Wallopers? thought Joel, weakly pulling out a packet of mints. Did that mean there were more of them? Or was he hallucinating?

He held out the packet. It promptly disappeared, paper and all.

"Er — what did you say you were?" inquired Joel, feeling foolish. (He only hoped no one was watching. But if you were going to hallucinate, you should know at least what it was you were hallucinating.)

"I is a walloper. Big furry walloper." The walloper crunched and swallowed. A look of surprise came over its face. "Huuuuuurgh," went the walloper, its mouth gaping open. It put up a paw and wafted peppermint fumes over Joel. "That's gooder," it said. "Where was us?"

"I was asking you what you were," said Joel politely.

"Did I told you?"

"You said you were a — a hairy walloper."

"Furry walloper. Yush. Big furry walloper. That's what I is. See?" The walloper pointed proudly to a medallion hanging around its neck. Joel leaned forward to read it.

Big furry walloper, said the medallion. *Harmless herbivore. Roams in hordes.* Now that he could see the rest of it, Joel discovered that the walloper was like a giant kangaroo with long hair.

"Where are the rest of you?" he said.

"Out there somewhere. Mooching around." The walloper reached down and began to rummage in its pouch. Joel couldn't decide whether it was scratching itself or searching for something. "That your toothbrush wot I just seen?"

"Toothbrush?" said Joel.

"Long stick with bristles on the end."

"Oh! You mean the broomstick. Yes," said Joel. "We flew here on it but it's not actually mine. It belongs," said Joel, carelessly, "to a friend of ours who's a wizard."

"Izzat so?" said the walloper, rummaging again. "Well, I be off now, then. Bye-bye!"

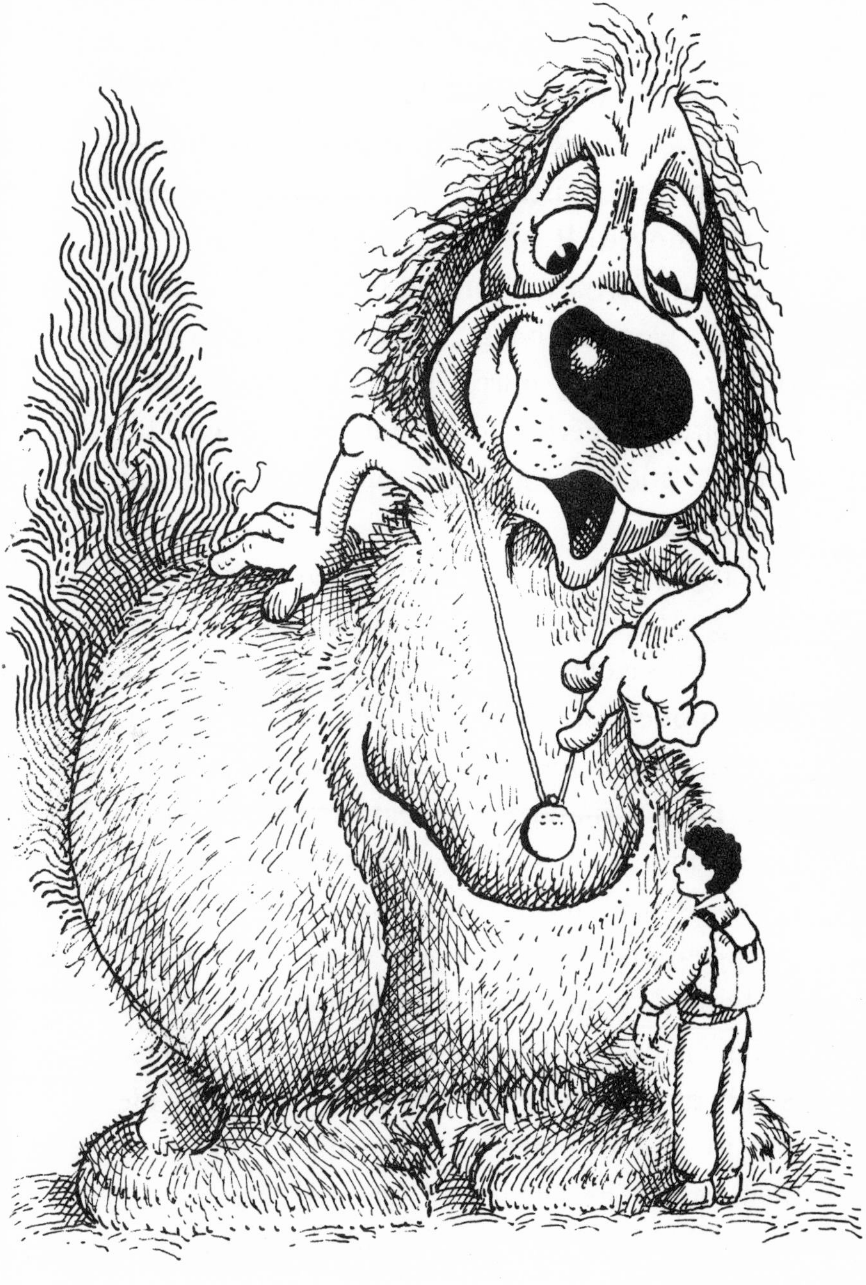

"Bye-bye," said Joel.

He stood watching as the walloper whumpfed away into the mist. The ground shook beneath it as it moved. It *seemed* to be real.

Thoughtfully, Joel turned back to the ladder. A man wearing baggy, knee-length shorts in violent shades of purple had just stepped onto the platform. Seeing Joel, he fell burbling to his knees, mouth gaping open and arms outstretched.

"Elvis!" he burbled. "Elvis, baby . . . sing to me!"

Joel looked nervously over his shoulder; there was no one there. The man was talking to *him*.

"My name's Joel," he said. "Not Elvis."

At this the man gave a great shriek, burst into tears, and went scuttling up the ladder. Joel could hear him, still babbling, as he disappeared: "Honey, I just seen Elvis! I just spoke with him! Lordy, Lordy! I've met Elvis!"

This is crazy, thought Joel. This whole place is full of loonies. He made for the ladder. He had to find Gemma and Ben-Muzzy and drag them out of here before it was too late.

He found them on the next platform. Gemma

was writhing and twisting as if she were in pain. Strangulated sounds were coming out of her mouth. "Ooby looby boo ba," she was singing. "Booby bee ba boo!"

Joel groaned. He knew what Gemma was dreaming. She was dreaming that she was Tracey Trotter. Tracey Trotter and the Porkers was her favorite group. Joel couldn't stand them. This was unbearable!

He looked around for Ben-Muzzy. It took him a moment or two to find him among the crowd of fellow dreamers, the reason being that Ben-Muzzy was fast becoming invisible. From the neck downward he was no longer there.

"This is ridiculous!" shouted Joel.

A woman nearby cried, "Daddy!"

"Oh, be quiet!" snapped Joel. He elbowed his way across to Gemma. "Stop that this instant!" he said, doing his best to sound like Miss Foster when she told off Graham Roberts for throwing paper darts.

"Boo bee doo dee doo!" sang Gemma, shimmying around in front of him.

A sense of despair began to creep over Joel. Great fun and adventure *this* was. What, with a

twin who thought she was a pop star and a
wizard who almost wasn't there?

"Hilloo!" said a familiar voice in the region of
his left ear.

Joel spun around.

"I thought you'd like to know," said the big furry walloper. "The Airy Fairies has stolen your broomstick. . . ."

Chapter Three

"Stolen our broomstick?" cried Joel.

"Yush." The walloper nodded. "They is playing wiv it. Up there." He waved a paw at the clouds. "I just thought this is something you would like to know. I'll say good-bye now. Bye-bye!"

Joel didn't wait to say good-bye back. He rushed to his twin, seized her by the arm, and screamed into her ear, "The Airy Fairies have stolen the broomstick!"

Gemma's eyes twinkled at him. "Dooby dooby doo dah!" sang Gemma happily.

Joel made an exasperated noise in the back of his throat. Still keeping a firm grip on Gemma, he dragged her over to the fast-disappearing

Ben-Muzzy. Only the tip of his hat was visible now.

"We've got to go!" bawled Joel into what he thought might be one of Ben-Muzzy's ears. "The Airy Fairies have stolen the broomstick!"

"Oh, Your Highness, Your Wizardship," babbled Ben-Muzzy. "Such an honor!"

"*Listen!*" bellowed Joel. He snatched a handful of air in the hope that part of it might be Ben-Muzzy. "Can you hear me? I said, *the Airy Fairies have stolen the broomstick!*"

"Ow!" yelped Ben-Muzzy. "You're hurting me slightly, Your Majesty!"

Joel clicked his tongue. Ruthlessly hauling his reluctant charges in his wake, he elbowed his way through little knots of people in various stages of delirium toward a sign that said EXIT. Someone tore at his track suit as he passed, someone else fell to the ground and started licking his feet.

This is horrible! thought Joel.

The main exit was through a door marked HAPPY LANDINGS, but there was also a trapdoor in the floor of the platform that said RUDE AWAKENINGS: FOR EMERGENCY USE ONLY.

If this wasn't an Emergency, thought Joel, he'd like to know what was. He yanked up the trap and bundled first Gemma, and then Ben-Muzzy, into the darkness beyond. It was like putting packages down a chute, except that packages didn't wriggle and kick and sing stupid songs.

"Beeby booby doo ba!" warbled Gemma as she shot out of sight. "Deeby dooby — OOPS!"

Gemma's singing broke off abruptly, followed almost immediately by a long howl of protest from Ben-Muzzy: "It's not time to get up!"

Rude Awakenings, thought Joel. Serves them right! Silly pair of idiots. He lowered himself cautiously through the trap, slammed it shut over his head, and went hurtling off into black space.

It was the strangest sensation! One minute he was wide awake, and the next he felt as if he were being roughly shaken out of a night's deep sleep.

"Gerroff!" shouted Joel. "Leave me alone!"

"What *is* the matter with you?" said Gemma.

Joel gasped. "I thought you were trying to get

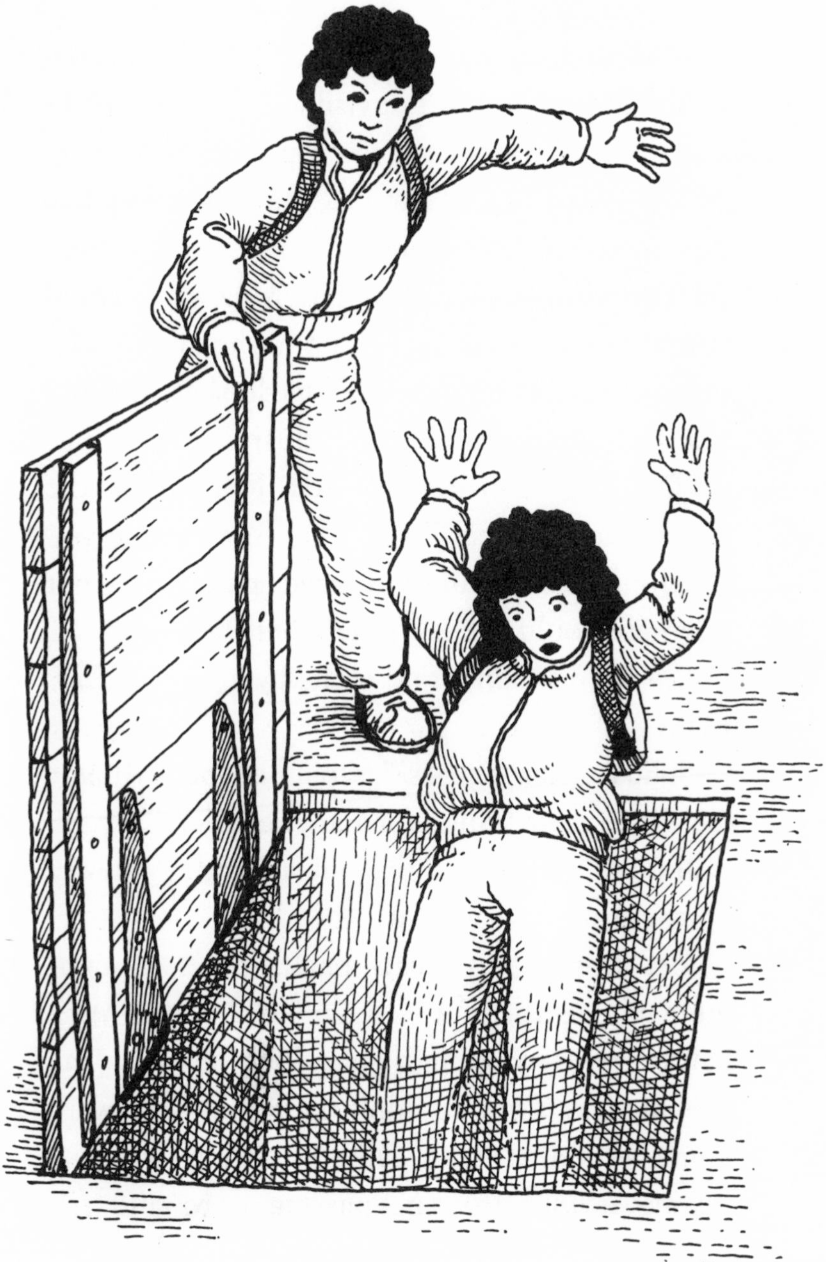

me out of bed! Where's Ben-Muzzy?"

Ben-Muzzy was still invisible — all except for a tiny black triangle at the top of his hat.

"Oh, dear!" said Gemma. She stifled a giggle. "He seems to have gone!"

"You can laugh," said Ben-Muzzy. "This is worrying! I've been woken up in the middle of a dream. You're not supposed to do that. Do you realize I could be *stuck* like this?"

"Do you realize," retorted Joel, "that the broomstick is gone?"

"Gone?" Ben-Muzzy turned pale (not that anybody could see). "Gone where?"

"It's been stolen," said Joel, "by a gang of Airy Fairies."

"Those Airy Fairies!" screamed Ben-Muzzy. "I'll have their wings for handkerchiefs!"

"Look!" Gemma flung out a hand. "They're up there playing with it!"

Joel tipped his head back. Sure enough, there above them was a whole flock of Airy Fairies twittering and squeaking around the broomstick. They couldn't fly it, but they were doing the next best thing, juggling with it, tossing it into the air, passing it to and fro among themselves.

"Hey!" shouted Ben-Muzzy, and the triangle at the tip of his hat wobbled in outrage. "You bring that broomstick back!"

The Airy Fairies took no notice.

"This is not funny," said Joel. "If they make off with it, how are we going to get home?"

Even as he spoke, a sudden gust of wind sent both broomstick and Airy Fairies scudding off in a different direction.

"You come back here!" thundered Ben-Muzzy, shaking an invisible fist; but the Airy Fairies only tittered. Gemma thought, but could not be sure, that she saw one of them actually stick out a tiny tongue.

"They're doing it deliberately," she said.

Ben-Muzzy gritted his teeth. "I told you they made nuisances of themselves."

"You shouldn't have been so mean to them."

"Mean?" said Ben-Muzzy. "I wasn't mean!"

"Yes you were. You flew right through them. Then you said they were brainless."

"Well, they are brainless! Look at them!" roared Ben-Muzzy. "Is that any way to treat a broomstick?"

A crowd of Airy Fairies had attached themselves to it and were riding along underneath. Some, showing off, were hanging on by one hand; others, showing off even more, had their legs hooked over and were dangling upside down. Some were dancing along the top of it, some turning cartwheels, some using it to play leapfrog. Every now and again, as the twins and Ben-Muzzy stood helplessly watching, the wind would whirl them around in little eddies, or whisk them higher up into the clouds. If somebody didn't do something, thought Joel, they would soon be whisked right out of sight.

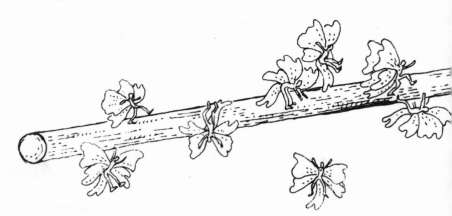

"We'll have to go after them," he said.

"How?" wailed Gemma.

Joel turned pointedly to look at Ben-Muzzy. He was supposed to be a wizard.

"No use looking at me," said Ben-Muzzy. And indeed it wasn't, all things considered. You might as well gaze at empty space as gaze at an invisible person. "*I* can't do anything. Being woken up like that has drained away all my magic.

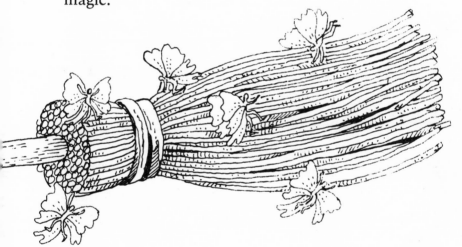

It could take ages to come back. By then they'll have lost interest and dumped it anywhere, knowing that Airy Fairy crew."

"Where do they live?" said Joel, frowningly watching as the Airy Fairies tumbled and rolled, sliding up and down the air currents with their new toy.

"They don't live anywhere. They just go with the wind. They are totally irresponsible."

It could be argued, reflected Joel, that Ben-Muzzy had been totally irresponsible leaving the broomstick unguarded, but it was a little late for recriminations. What they needed was — A walloper! A big furry walloper!

"Hey!" yelled Joel.

A herd of wallopers cropping the grass nearby obligingly raised their baggy heads and turned, chewing, in his direction. So they *were* real! He had had a horrible feeling that he might have dreamed them.

"They look like nice animals," said Gemma.

"They're brainless," said Ben-Muzzy.

"You say everything's brainless!"

"Wallopers are specially brainless. They are noted for their brainlessness. They are possibly," said Ben-Muzzy, "the only creatures in the known universe to have nothing inside their skulls."

One of the wallopers had detached itself from the rest of the herd and was thumping amiably toward them, rummaging in its pouch as it came.

"Hilloo!" it said. "Does I know you?"

"You might," said Joel. It was hard to tell one walloper from another. They all had medallions hanging around their necks. "Was it you who told us about the Airy Fairies stealing our broomstick?"

"It might have been," said the walloper. It opened its pouch and looked inside. It was a very large and roomy pouch, like a big trash bag — and it was empty. "Empty," said the walloper.

"Hey! I've got an idea!" cried Joel.

Gemma had the same idea.

"I wonder," she said with a winning smile, "whether it would be possible for you to give us a lift?"

"Just a little ride in your pouch," said Joel. "You don't mind having passengers, do you?"

Without waiting for the walloper to say yes or no, Joel hopped inside, followed quickly by Gemma and the tip of Ben-Muzzy's hat.

"Ooo," said the walloper. "Tickles."

"What a positively *incredible* notion!" breathed Gemma.

Joel stood up and stuck his head out of the pouch. "Quick," he snapped. "Follow that broomstick!"

The walloper liked following the broomstick. It thought it was some kind of game. Happily it galumphed over hill and dale, and as it galumphed it whimbled to itself. "Follow a broomstick," whimbled the walloper. "Big furry walloper, following a broomstick."

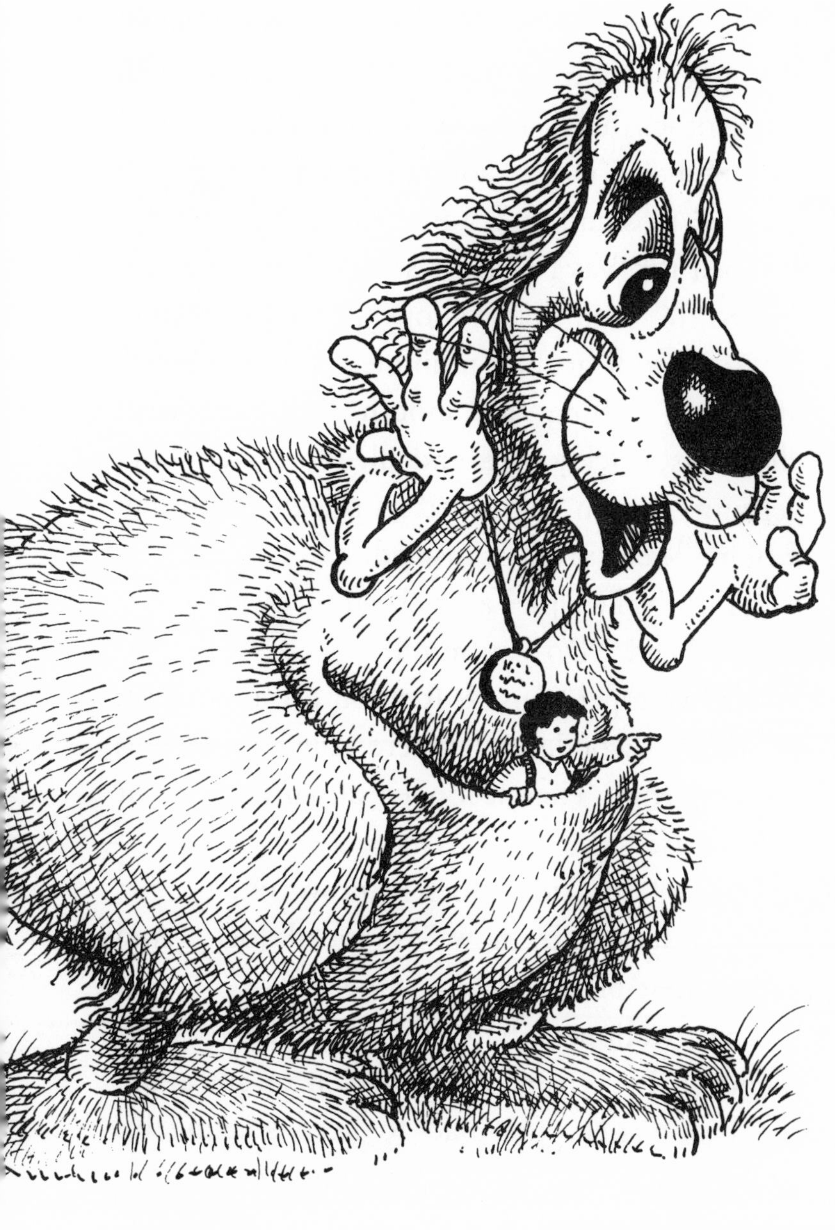

The only problem was that every few seconds, it stopped following the broomstick and started doing other things instead. Sometimes it stopped to rummage in its pouch, sometimes it just stopped to stand and stare. But mostly what it stopped for was to eat. It seemed there was no end to the food that wallopers could consume.

"All good grub," mumbled the walloper, absently stuffing its mouth full of sweet chestnuts, prickly parts and all. When it couldn't get any more in, it opened its pouch and began lobbing them in there instead.

"Hey!" yelled Joel as a chestnut cracked him on the head. "Do you mind?"

The walloper paused. It stood for a moment, obviously wondering where the voice was coming from. Then it looked down with an air of surprise.

"Hilloo!" it said. "Does I know you?"

"You should by now!" snapped Joel. "And follow that broomstick!"

The walloper had a remarkably short memory. Every time it stopped, it forgot about the broomstick. Joel had to keep sticking his head over the edge of the pouch to remind it. In the end, he decided it was simpler to stay with his head outside, and after a while Gemma and Ben-Muzzy joined him. Gemma said it made her feel sick, being bounced along at the bottom of a stuffy old pouch. Ben-Muzzy said that some air would be a fine thing.

"About time this animal took a bath," he grumbled, and, "Watch what you're doing!" he added as a great horny fingernail came rummaging around into the pouch and nearly scraped his ear off.

"Is I hearing something?" said the walloper. It stopped and looked down again. "Hilloo!" it said. "Does I know you?"

Gemma giggled. Ben-Muzzy groaned. Joel, growing agitated, shouted, *"The broomstick!"*

A flurry of wind had caught the Airy Fairies and was carrying them off at full speed. Higher and higher they flew, farther and farther, until they were the merest speck in the sky.

"Oh, quick!" begged Gemma. "Please!"

The walloper, ever eager to oblige, set off at a gallop. *Whumpf, whumpf, whumpf,* went the walloper, clearing whole fields at a single bound. The earth beneath it trembled. Ben-

Muzzy and the twins clung in terror to the edge of the pouch.

In the distance loomed a hill. The walloper reached it in a couple of bounds. Another bound and it was halfway up.

"Haaaaa . . . *WHUMPF!*" went the walloper, kicking up its heels.

"He-e-e-e-elp!" screamed Gemma as she was catapulted out of the pouch.

Ben-Muzzy and Joel were catapulted with her. The walloper walloped on, mindless and happy. By the time it reached the far side of the hill, it would forget that it had ever had anything but a handful of sweet chestnuts in its pouch. As for the broomstick, that had disappeared.

Chapter Four

"Ow!" cried Gemma as she landed on something hard.

"Watch out!" yelled Joel, catapulting past.

Cautiously, Gemma picked herself up. Beneath her she could feel cold, dank rocks and some kind of slimy moss. All around was a thick brown mist that hovered and hung. The mist smelled like sewers and rotten eggs. It seemed to be seeping out of the ground.

"Where is everybody?" wailed Gemma.

"I'm here," said Joel. "Where's Ben-Muzzy?"

"Over here," said Ben-Muzzy's voice. There was the sound of slithering and sliding, and then the tip of Ben-Muzzy's hat could be seen bobbing through the mist. "This really is too bad!" grumbled Ben-Muzzy. "Trust a walloper! I told you they were brainless. I told —"

"Sh!" Gemma held up a hand. "I can hear something!"

All three held their breath and listened. From somewhere underground came a low rumbling of voices. Then a light appeared, and then another and another, until there were at least a dozen of them. As the lights came nearer, Gemma was able to make out a crowd of small humpbacked creatures, all gnarled and knotted like the trunks of trees, advancing upon them with lanterns and pitchforks. Narrow, red-rimmed eyes glittered malevolently out of faces as wrinkled and shriveled as old potatoes. Their noses were like great leathery doorknobs, and their long yellowing beards were matted with pieces of stale food.

"What are they?" whispered Gemma. They seemed to be wearing some kind of uniform — brown hoods with yellow tunics, and leggings bound with creepers. Gemma shivered. She didn't like the look of them. They looked like gnomes.

The gnomes were now surrounding them,

holding up their lanterns to get a better view. After a short silence one of the leading gnomes said, "Take them below!" and the twins found themselves being bundled toward an opening in the rocks.

"Stop it, you're hurting me!" shrieked Gemma as one of her captors jabbed her with the pronged stick he was carrying. The gnome only sniggered and jabbed her again.

Gemma clutched Joel's hand as together they were driven down a steep flight of steps carved out of the rock. Where was Ben-Muzzy? she wondered. The gnomes wouldn't have seen him, invisible as he was. Had they left him outside?

At the bottom of the steps was a long, low tunnel, dimly lit by lanterns hanging from the ceiling. The twins were pushed along it. Every so often they passed parties of working gnomes, lugging buckets of water or digging holes. All the gnomes stopped what they were doing and examined the captives curiously, poking at them with sticklike fingers, pulling their hair, or tweaking their noses.

At the end of the tunnel, they came to a large underground hall where rows of gnomes were

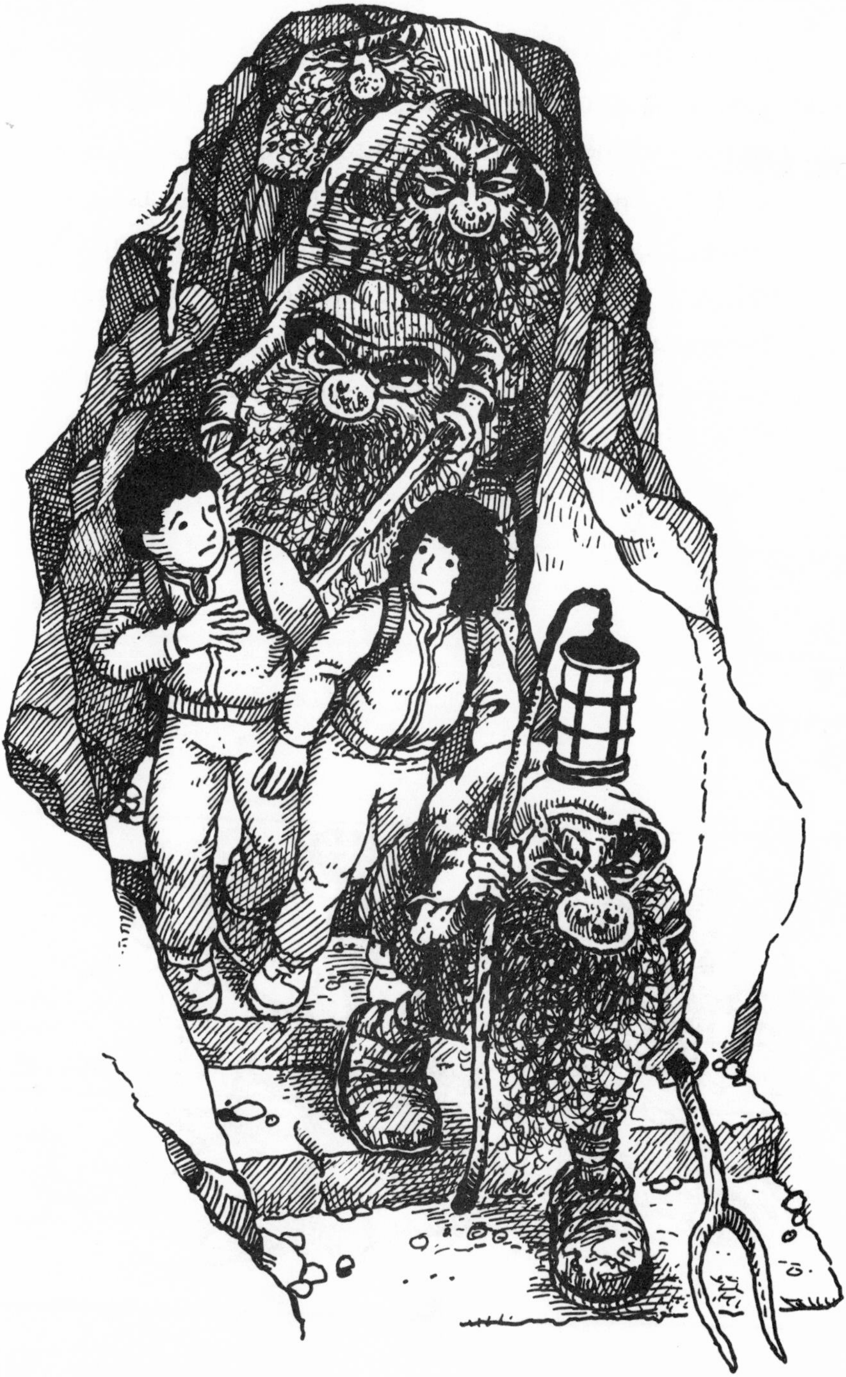

sitting at two long tables, being served food by other gnomes wearing white aprons. Gemma couldn't quite make out what the food was. It seemed to be a kind of black and sticky soup, and she was almost sure she had seen one gnome eating beetles.

The twins were marched across the hall and through a wooden door, into a musty-smelling

chamber where another gnome was sitting on a stone seat, combing his beard with a piece of twig. His hood was decorated with jays' feathers and his suit was made of fur. The twins were pushed to their knees. One of the gnomes who had captured them stepped forward and saluted.

"These are the spies, Your Overlord. We found them spying near the main entrance."

"We were not spying!" Joel said indignantly. "We were just sitting up there minding our own business."

The Overlord stopped combing his beard and looked down at the twins. "How many of you are there?"

Joel was about to say, "Just the three of us," when he remembered that Ben-Muzzy, wherever he was, was invisible apart from the tip of his hat.

"Two of us," he said. "You can see there are two of us, can't you? Don't you know how to count?"

One of the gnomes jabbed him in the ribs with his pronged stick. Joel yelled. The Overlord leaned forward.

"Don't you get smart with me," he said. "We know who you are. You've been sent as spies by the Green Elves."

"We are not spies!" roared Joel.

"We came from Wonderland," said Gemma. "By accident. We sort of fell over the edge, if you know what I mean."

"I do not know what you mean," said the Overlord. "In any case, you're obviously lying. Spies always lie." He snapped his fingers. "Take them away and put them with the other spy."

Joel and Gemma were pulled to their feet, pushed out into the tunnel once again, and prodded and poked down another flight of steps. The steps seemed to go on forever. They were steep and winding and cut right into the heart of the earth.

"In there!" said one of the gnomes, unlocking a stout wooden door. "Get in!"

"Why?" said Joel. "What are you going to do with us?"

The gnome cackled hoarsely. "What we always do to spies . . . roast them alive, and then eat them!"

The door slammed shut and was locked, leaving the twins in darkness. They heard the gnomes scuffling back up the tunnel.

For a few seconds they held on to each other very tightly and said nothing; then, they slowly became aware of a curious green glow in the far corner of the dungeon.

"What is it?" whispered Gemma.

Bravely, Joel took a step toward it. At the center of the light, all hunched up, was a little spindly creature, needle-thin and semitransparent, with huge saucer-shaped eyes glowing green in the darkness. Joel and Gemma stared at it wonderingly.

"Excuse me, but you're not by any chance a Green Elf?" asked Joel, seeing the delicate wings that sprouted from its back.

The little creature nodded. "Yes," it said, and its voice was high and silvery like a tiny bell. "Who are you?"

"We're twins," said Gemma. "I'm Gemma and this is my brother Joel. We've just been taken prisoner by these hateful gnome-things." She squatted by the side of the elf. "What's your name?"

"Teeno," said the elf. "Why have they taken you prisoner?"

"'Cause they say we're spies." Joel sank down cross-legged, on the floor beside Gemma. "I don't s'pose *you're* a spy, are you?"

Teeno drooped his head. "I was sent here to find out what they were planning."

"And what are they planning?" said Gemma.

"I don't know." Two tears formed in Teeno's eyes. "I was caught almost the minute I got here."

"Oh dear," said Gemma. Her voice wobbled in sympathy. "And it doesn't seem at all a nice sort of place to be."

"It isn't," said Teeno. Slowly the tears spilled over and went trickling down his cheeks, sparkling and shining like drops of crystal. "This is the home of the Paddiwack Gnomes. No one ever gets out alive. But one of the Laughing Pixies told us that the Paddiwacks were planning to attack us, and our Queen asked for someone to come and find out if it was true."

"How long have you been here?" asked Gemma.

"I've lost count of the days," said Teeno. "Weeks, I think."

"But what are they going to do with you?"

"Use me as a tablecloth," said Teeno, and this time a whole cascade of teardrops went rolling down his cheeks.

"Pardon me, but did you say a *table*cloth?" said Gemma.

"For the Overlord's table. That's what they do with Green Elves . . . they don't eat us, they say there isn't anything on us. So they sew us together to make tablecloths. It takes a thousand Green Elves to make one tablecloth and the Overlord's already got two."

"That's *terrible!*" said Gemma.

"Yes, and the worst of it is, they have to starve us first. When we're starved, we get transparent. That's what they like."

"Are they starving you now?" said Gemma.

"Look at me," said Teeno. "Can you see through me yet?"

Gemma peered. "Not quite. But nearly."

"That's because they haven't given me anything to eat since I've been here."

"We've got food," said Gemma. "Would you like some? There's fruit and chocolate cake and sandwiches."

"I'd love some," said Teeno, clasping his tiny hands together. "What are sandwiches and chocolate cake?"

Gemma spread them out for inspection. Teeno gasped.

"That would feed the whole of our kingdom for months!" he said. "I've never seen so much food!"

"Help yourself," said Joel generously.

The sight of sandwiches had made Joel hungry. He hoped Teeno wouldn't eat everything, though of course he should have as much as he wanted.

"I wouldn't mind some of that," said Teeno, pointing to the chocolate cake. He scooped up a small handful of crumbs. "Is it all right to eat all this?"

He ate up all the crumbs and a corner of a sandwich and had a few sips of orange juice from the cap on the bottle.

"Are you sure that's enough?" asked Joel anxiously. When Teeno assured him that it was, Joel said, "Well, we don't want everything to go stale," and began cramming the remains of the cake into his mouth as fast as he could. Gemma ate three sandwiches and felt large and greedy.

"What do elves usually eat?" she asked.

"Rose-hip syrup and honey that the bees make for us," said Teeno. He was looking more cheerful now, and not quite so transparent. "I feel much better after all that food," he told the twins. "And I'm very sorry they've taken you prisoner, but I can't help being glad that you're here. It's not quite so frightening when there's someone to talk to."

"What we should do," said Joel, "is start thinking how to escape."

Teeno shook his head sadly. "You can't

escape," he said. "The door's locked and there's no way out."

"There's always a way out," said Joel. He was a great reader of adventure stories. "For instance, we could — we could dig a tunnel!"

"How?" said Gemma. The floor of the dungeon was solid rock. Not even Joel could think of a way to dig through solid rock.

"There's only one thing to do," he said. "We'll just have to hope Ben-Muzzy finds us before they decide to roast us alive."

"Who's Ben-Muzzy?" asked Teeno.

"An invisible wizard," said Gemma.

"A wizard!" Teeno beat his hands together, making a tiny clapping sound. "He'll be able to cast spells on all the Paddiwacks and rescue us!"

Joel gave a hollow laugh. "I wouldn't bank on it," he said.

"I'm sure he'll do his best," said Gemma. "P'raps we should start singing songs to cheer him on?"

"What'll we sing?"

Gemma thought for a moment. Her face brightened. "Beeby dooby bah bee!" sang Gemma, snapping her fingers.

"*No,*" said Joel.

Gemma sulked. Then she said, "I know! I know what we'll sing! We'll sing one of his spells. We'll sing the spell he did that time you got changed into a puddle of mud . . .

Iggly oogly wubbly ub,
Into a boy this puddle of mud.
Iggly oogly wubbly in,
Change it back to Gemma's twin."

Neither of the twins had a particularly tuneful voice, but at least they were loud. If Ben-Muzzy were anywhere at all in the Caves of the Paddiwack Gnomes, he would surely be able to hear them.

Ben-Muzzy was at a loss what to do when the gnomes started dragging Joel and Gemma away. For a moment he thought of trying to fight them and pull the twins to safety, but he had nothing to fight them with, and besides there were dozens of gnomes and only one of Ben-Muzzy, even if he was invisible.

He crouched by the side of a large rock,

watching as the twins were driven underground. Had his magic come back he could have said a spell to make the twins invisible, too, but he knew from the tingling in his toes that it still had a long way to go. It hadn't reached his ankles yet; if he could produce a mouse from a top hat he'd be lucky.

On the other hand, *he* was invisible. Invisible all over, apart from the tip of his hat, and if anyone noticed a small piece of hat moving through the air, they would never guess there was a wizard underneath it.

Ben-Muzzy decided that what he must do was follow and see where the twins were taken. Then he could work out a plan.

Bold in his invisibleness, Ben-Muzzy walked over to the crack in the rocks and went down a flight of stone steps. At the bottom was a door. Ben-Muzzy tried the handle, but the door was locked on the inside. He rapped loudly with his knuckles.

"Who is it?" demanded a voice on the other side.

Ben-Muzzy rapped again, louder. There was a jangling of keys, and then the door was hauled open and a gnome peered out.

"Who is it?" he said, jabbing the air with his pronged stick.

Ben-Muzzy doubled himself up, ducked under the gnome's arm, and crawled through into a dark tunnel. The gnome swung a lantern high into the air. He muttered to himself and slammed the door angrily. "Some stupid pixie playing jokes."

Ben-Muzzy hurried on down the tunnel. He passed a party of gnomes picking mushrooms and heard them talking about two prisoners. The twins?

In his excitement, not looking where he was going, Ben-Muzzy bumped into a gnome carrying a bucket of water. The water spilled over the ground, and the gnome swung around angrily.

"Who did that?" he cried. "Who spilled my water?"

There was no reply. The gnome stared around him, his jaw dropping open. Ben-Muzzy scurried onward.

At last he came to a big hall where rows of gnomes sat at two long tables. Ben-Muzzy skulked in the shadows and wondered what to do. The hall was brightly lit with lanterns hanging from the ceiling. Someone was sure to notice the tip of his hat moving through the air. Once they noticed it, they would try to find out what it was. And when they tried to find out what it was, they would discover there was a wizard underneath it. Even if they couldn't see Ben-Muzzy, they would be able to feel him.

Ben-Muzzy thought hard. He didn't like the idea of leaving his hat behind, because wizards' hats are magic and you never knew when you might need one for a spell.

As Ben-Muzzy stood hesitating, a gnome dressed in a blood-splattered apron came out of a nearby cave and staggered into the hall carrying a bucket full of what looked like crushed beetles. Ben-Muzzy watched as he worked his way up the first table, sploshing beetle mush out of a bucket with a big wooden ladle. Suddenly he knew what to do.

He waited until the cook came back for another bucketful, then tiptoed after him into the kitchens, took off his hat and stuffed it tip downward into the large pocket at the front of the cook's apron. The cook, refilling his bucket from a disgusting black pot simmering on an open stove, was far too busy to notice anything. The hat was now completely hidden.

Ben-Muzzy trotted back into the hall beside the cook. The gnomes were talking excitedly to each other as they stuffed their mouths. Ben-Muzzy learned that two spies had been brought in and had been taken down to the dungeons. He also learned that the gnomes were planning an attack on the Green Elves.

"Green Elves are no fun," grumbled one gnome, dribbling crushed beetles all down his beard. "Stupid little creatures. Die of fright as soon as look at you. I'd rather have a chance at the Laughing Pixies again . . . I like wiping the smiles off their silly faces."

"Ah, but this time it's going to be different," said another gnome, whose hands were covered in huge, hairy warts. "All those who don't die of fright are going to be brought back here to work for us. Every gnome that joins in the attack is going to be given a Green Elf as his own personal slave. His Overlord has said so . . . he's got enough tablecloths, he said. So now we're going to use them as slave labor instead."

The cook reached the end of the table and poured out the last of his beetle stew. As he turned to go back, Ben-Muzzy stretched out a hand and snatched his hat.

"What's that?" cried the cook.

Ben-Muzzy darted for the exit. The tip of his hat could clearly be seen, bouncing through the

air. The cook gave a yell, dropped his empty
bucket, and set off in pursuit. All the gnomes
jumped up from their chairs and ran after him.

Ben-Muzzy raced along a dark tunnel and
pressed himself hard into a corner. The gnomes

swarmed past him, shouting and pushing. Some were carrying knives and forks, and some of the knives and forks jabbed Ben-Muzzy painfully in the ribs. Ben-Muzzy bit his lip and bravely remained silent.

After a while, the gnomes came surging back up the tunnel.

"It was a black thing," said one. "A black thing moving through the air."

"It was enormous," said another. "Like a giant bat."

"Bigger than a bat," protested a third. "More like an eagle. Or even two eagles. Why, I even heard their wings flapping."

Eagles! thought Ben-Muzzy. These gnomes were idiots.

He turned and walked on down the tunnel. Before long he came to another flight of steps, going deep down into the heart of the earth; and from afar, as he stood there, he heard singing. The singing was very faint (and very out of tune) but Ben-Muzzy recognized the words immediately.

"Iggly oogly wubbly ub,
Into a boy this puddle of mud.
Iggly oogly wubbly in,
Change it back to Gemma's twin."

It was Joel and Gemma! They were trying to tell

him where they were!

Ben-Muzzy dashed helter-skelter down the steps. He was almost at the bottom when he caught his foot in his cloak, lost his balance, and went tumbling head over heels.

"What's that?"

A gnome came running up the tunnel, waving a lantern over his head.

"Who's there?" He peered suspiciously. (Ben-Muzzy's hat had fortunately rolled into a dark corner.) "Who made that noise?"

Ben-Muzzy side-stepped. He looked at the gnome and his eyes brightened. Hanging from a belt around his waist was a large bunch of keys.

Carefully, the gnome began to probe the ground, prodding and poking into the dark corners with his pronged stick. Ben-Muzzy dodged out of the way, watching for his opportunity. As soon as the gnome turned his back, Ben-Muzzy made a grab. The gnome leapt around.

"Wha——"

Boff! went Ben-Muzzy. The gnome fell sprawling, and the lantern flew from his hands.

Instantly Ben-Muzzy snatched the keys, seized the pronged stick, wrenched it from the gnome's grasp, and began jabbing at him fiercely.

With a screech of terror the gnome scrambled to his feet and made a dive for the steps. That would teach him, thought Ben-Muzzy, picking up his hat. It took a wizard to put these gnomes in their place.

Ben-Muzzy hurried on along the tunnel.

"Iggly oogly wubbly in," chanted the twins.

"Pst!" said Ben-Muzzy. "Pst, pst!"

"Is that you?" whispered Joel excitedly.

"Yes," whispered Ben-Muzzy.

"We've got a Green Elf with us," squeaked Gemma's voice through the keyhole. "He's called Teeno and he's been here for days and —"

"Sh!" said Ben-Muzzy. "Stop talking!"

One after another, Ben-Muzzy tried the keys in the lock. On the other side of the door, Joel clenched his fists and Gemma chewed her fingernails while the Green Elf danced up and down, whirring his tiny wings.

"Quickly, quickly!" urged Gemma.

"I'm doing my best," panted Ben-Muzzy.

He tried the very last key of all. The door

swung open, and as it did so there came the heavy tramping of feet down the tunnel. The gnomes were coming to investigate!

The twins and Teeno hustled out of the dungeon. Ben-Muzzy gave them a shove.

"That way! I don't know where it goes, but there are gnomes up the other way."

"What about you?" hissed Gemma.

"I'll be all right, they can't see me . . . here! Take this!"

Ben-Muzzy bundled his hat into Gemma's arms. Joel grabbed her hand and the twins raced off, with Teeno flickering at their heels. Ben-Muzzy waited by the dungeon door . . .

The gnomes arrived in a pack, headed by a particularly horrible gnome who looked as if he had the chicken pox.

"The door's open!" exclaimed Chicken Pox.

He hurried through it, swinging his lantern to light up the dark corners. The other gnomes swarmed in after him, all except for one who remained, baffled, peering down the tunnel.

"That way! They've gone that way!" he shouted, but before he could take off in pursuit, Ben-Muzzy had given him a mighty push through the door.

"Aaaaaaaaagh!" screamed the gnome, crashing into his companions, who were on their way out. The whole pack went tumbling back into the dungeon.

Ben-Muzzy promptly slammed the door on them, locked it, and put the keys in his pocket.

Then he picked up his cloak and tore down the tunnel after the twins and Teeno.

If the tunnel led back to the open air, they might have a chance of escaping. But if it came to a dead end, he knew they would all be captured. For by now, every single gnome in the caves would be on the lookout for them.

Chapter Five

"I have — got — the most — awful — stitch," panted Gemma.

"Can't help that," puffed Joel. "Where's Ben-Muzzy?"

"Here!" Ben-Muzzy's voice echoed eerily up the tunnel. Gemma stopped and turned and felt a body bump into her.

"If that's you," said Gemma, "would you like your hat back?"

An invisible hand reached out and took it from her.

"Keep moving!" snapped Ben-Muzzy.

The tunnel was narrow and rocky, sloping steeply uphill. While the twins and Ben-Muzzy slipped and scrambled, Teeno darted ahead, a flickering green light in the gloom. His wings were not powerful enough for him to fly, but they whirred around like tiny propellers, skimming him across the floor.

After a while, the floor of the tunnel rose so sharply, and the roof came down so low, that they had to drop to their hands and knees and crawl — all except Teeno, who was small enough to stand without bumping his head.

Ben-Muzzy prodded urgently at Gemma. "Go faster! I think they're coming after us!"

They crawled on as quickly as they could, scraping their knees on the rocky floor. The gnomes were not far behind. Their heavy boots could be heard clumping and clattering.

Gemma was out of breath again. Her heart was thumping against her ribs and her stitch had come back.

Suddenly there was a squeak of excitement from Teeno: "I can smell air!" And then another squeak: "I can see daylight!"

They had come right up to the surface, to a narrow opening in the rock. Teeno slipped through without any trouble, but Joel got a foot stuck and Gemma had to wrench off his shoe before he was able to pull himself free. All the time, behind them, they could hear the lumbering footsteps of the gnomes growing closer.

"Quick!" yelped Ben-Muzzy.

Gemma shoved Joel's sneaker up through the crack and wriggled herself after it. Ben-Muzzy pushed her from behind and Joel pulled her from above. For a moment Gemma thought she was going to break in half, and then she was out, in the fresh air, with the scent of flowers and the smell of grass. It was wonderful after the musty gloom of the caves.

The tip of Ben-Muzzy's hat appeared through the crack. Joel stretched out to help and groped around until he found a hand.

"Ow!" squawked Ben-Muzzy. "Ouch! Help! My cloak's caught!"

By now they could hear the shouts of the advancing gnomes. There was a long tearing sound, and then the tip of Ben-Muzzy's hat rose into the air. At the same time, two scrawny arms came snaking through the crack. Gemma saw them and gave a stifled screech. Joel, less squeamish than his twin, promptly stamped on

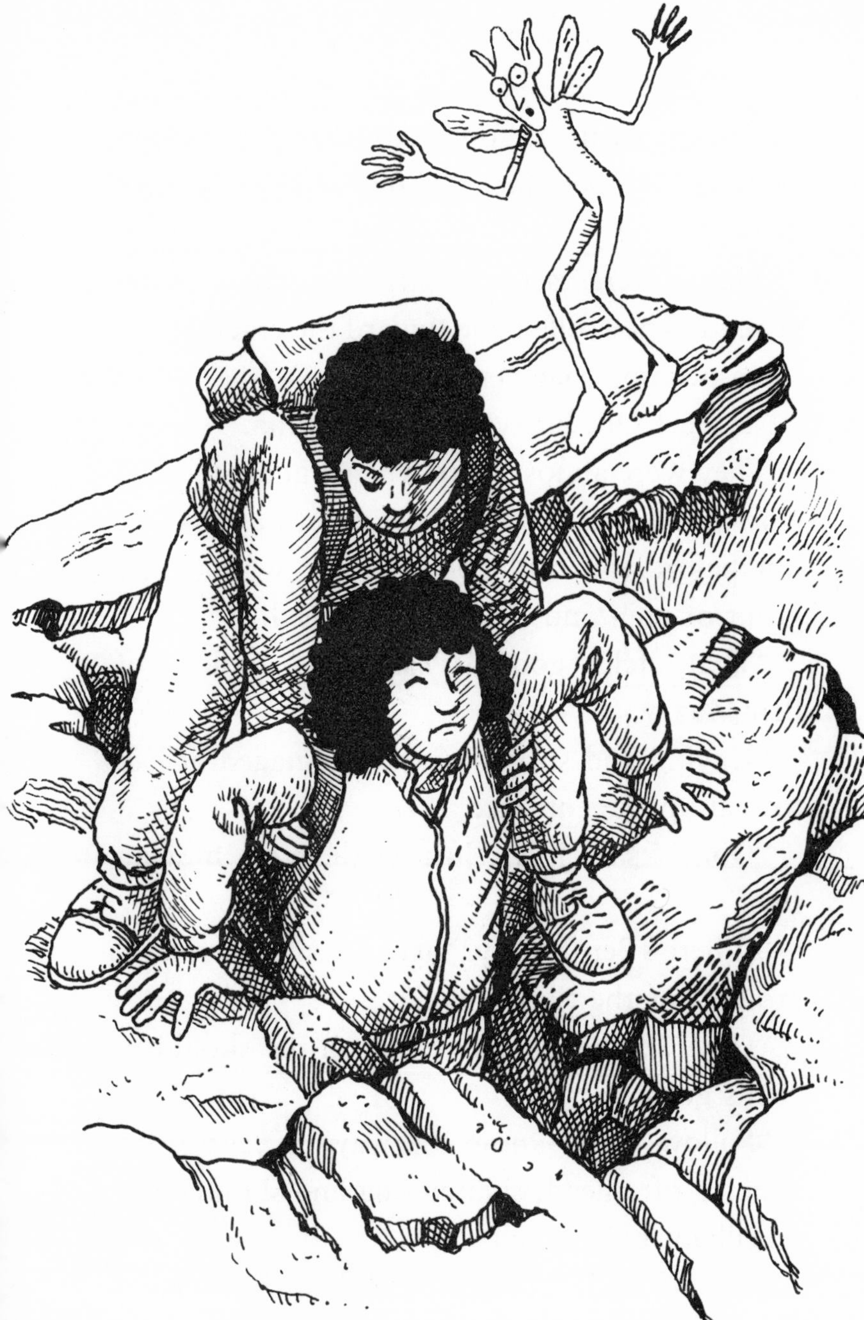

them. The arms disappeared.

"Quick!" cried Joel. "Shove something over it!"

There were several large boulders lying around. They rolled one toward the crack, all of them pushing together.

"Hurry! Oh, hurry!" urged Gemma.

They were almost there when a gnome's head emerged. Gemma opened her mouth to scream, but before she could do so there was a loud grunt of pain and the head vanished.

"That felt good!" said the voice of Ben-Muzzy.

Heaving and straining, they managed at last to seal up the entrance.

"Done!" said Joel. "Just let them try moving *that!*"

"Where's Ben-Muzzy?" asked Gemma, looking around for the tip of his hat.

"Here." A hand tapped her on the shoulder. "Let's go!"

"Follow me! I know the way!" Teeno went dancing off ahead, shimmering and shining like a brilliant green firefly.

The mist rolled away behind them. They were

in a land of flowers and sunshine. Birds chirped in the trees and bees bumbled busily as they collected pollen. Insects scurried to and fro in the grass, squirrels counted up the nuts they had stored, a frog sat sunning itself on the bank of a pool. Just like a picture book, thought Gemma.

Teeno led the way, through the Dark Forest, past the Lair of the Laughing Pixies, safely around the edge of the Bubbling Bog where the Hobgoblins hung out, across the Shining Stream where the Water Sprites played, on tiptoe past the Den of the Daredevil Dwarfs, until they came at last to the Grove of the Green Elves, where all day long the elves frolicked in the sunshine.

"You can come in," said Teeno. "They won't be scared if you're with me."

The twins and Ben-Muzzy stepped carefully, afraid of crushing the tiny creatures that gathered around, all beating their hands in excitement and exclaiming in high, silvery voices. Teeno pushed his way importantly through their midst.

"I'll take you to the Queen," he said.

The Queen was sitting on a large red toadstool, rocking a baby elf in a cradle made of cobwebs. On her head she wore a daisy-chain crown, her slippers were made of the softest foxglove, and her green leaf dress was decorated with hundreds of sparkling raindrops.

Teeno prostrated himself before her. Gemma, after some hesitation, dropped a curtsy. She knew it must have looked rather silly, when she was wearing a track suit which now had holes in both knees, but one had to do something in the presence of royalty.

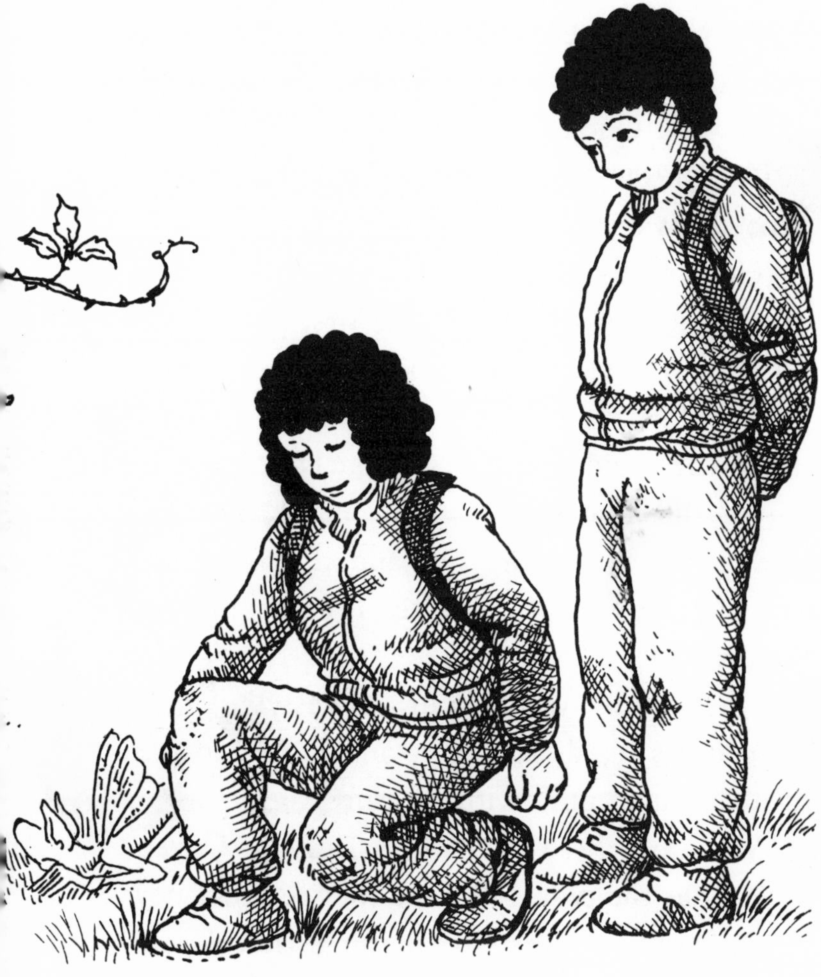

Joel, feeling foolish, just nodded his head and remained standing. He had no intention of groveling before a Green Elf who hardly came up to his kneecaps, even if she was a Queen.

"Oh, Your Majesty," said Teeno breathlessly, "I'm sorry I've been away so long, but I was locked up in a dungeon in the Caves of the Paddiwack Gnomes."

The Queen shivered and went on rocking the baby in its cobweb cradle.

"How perfectly dreadful!" she said. "Whatever made you go there in the first place?"

"If Your Majesty remembers," gasped Teeno, "Your Majesty sent me there to spy on them."

"Did I?" said the Queen vaguely. "I wonder why I did that? Well, never mind, I'm sure it was very brave of you, and if you remind me tomorrow, I shall give a party in your honor."

"Oh, thank you, Your Majesty!" Teeno clasped his hands together, and his green face turned almost pink with pleasure.

"Who are these people?" asked the Queen, looking at the twins. "I hope they're not a new kind of goblin come to live in the district. I don't care for goblins."

"Oh, Your Majesty, these aren't goblins," said Teeno, still in his lowly position on the grass. "These are twins, and they rescued me from the Paddiwacks. And that —" he pointed to the tip of Ben-Muzzy's hat —"that's an invisible wizard."

"Really?" said the Queen. "How very interesting. I've never seen an invisible wizard before." She peered in the direction of Ben-Muzzy. "I can't quite make him out, but I suppose he must be there if you say so."

"Your Majesty," said Ben-Muzzy, and he bowed right down till the tip of his hat touched the ground.

"Fascinating!" said the Queen. "You must all stay to tea!"

"Oh, thank you, Your Majesty," said Gemma, dropping another curtsy.

Joel just grunted.

The Queen leaned forward and idly tickled the baby elf under the chin. "I've forgotten," she said to Teeno. "Why did you say you went to the Paddiwack Caves?"

"Oh, Your Majesty, Your Majesty sent me

there as a spy," said Teeno earnestly. "Your Majesty wanted me to find out if the Paddiwacks were going to attack us."

"And were they?" said the Queen, smothering a yawn.

"Well, Your Majesty —"

Teeno hesitated, and Ben-Muzzy cleared his throat.

"As a matter of fact," he said, "Your Majesty," he added, "I overheard the gnomes saying they were planning to attack as soon as night fell. They said they were going to capture all the Green Elves and take them back to the Caves. They said —"

Ben-Muzzy got no further. The Queen had jumped up with a loud scream, overturning the baby elf's cradle. Teeno leapt to his feet, his face pale green.

"The Paddiwacks are coming!" The Queen ran distractedly this way and that, wringing her hands. "The Paddiwacks are coming, the Paddiwacks are coming!"

The news spread quickly among the other Green Elves. Soon they were all scurrying around in dozens of different directions. The

Queen's cry was taken up: "The Paddiwacks are coming, the Paddiwacks are coming!"

"Aren't you going to *do* something?" said Joel, looking at Teeno. "Don't you have an army?"

Teeno hung his head. "Green Elves don't fight. We can only run away and hide."

"But if you run away and hide tonight," pointed out Joel, "they'll only come again tomorrow. Can't the Laughing Pixies help?"

"They helped us last time," said Teeno. "They said they weren't going to do it anymore. They said we must fight our own battles in the future. Oh dear, oh dear! This is dreadful! We shall all be turned into tablecloths! Help, help! The Paddiwacks are coming!"

Teeno was borne away by the mass of panic-stricken Green Elves. Gemma picked up the baby elf and set him in his cradle.

"Poor little thing," she said. "He'll be crushed if these silly elves don't watch out."

"Look at them all," said Joel. "Just running in circles . . . You'd think they'd make *some* kind of effort."

"They are pretty useless," agreed Gemma. "Perhaps *we* should stay and help."

"Us?" said Joel. "Have you gone crazy?"

"No, but one should do good deeds when one can," said Gemma, setting the baby elf on his thistledown pillow.

"Never mind doing good deeds," said Joel. "What about getting back home?"

"We've got loads of time. We don't have to be back until dinner."

"Yes, and if we don't find the broomstick, I

don't see how we're going to get back at all!"

"That's all right," said Gemma. "Ben-Muzzy can take us."

Ben-Muzzy? thought Joel. She must be crazy! (Even Ben-Muzzy, invisible as he was, shuffled a little nervously.)

"What do *you* think?" Gemma addressed herself to the space where she judged Ben-Muzzy to be. "Do you think we should stay and help or do you think we should go and try to find the broomstick?"

"What I think," said Ben-Muzzy glumly, "is that until my magic has come back, we're stuck here whether we like it or not."

He twitched his toes experimentally. "It's only just about reached as far as my knees."

"Well, there you are," said Gemma. "That's it. We'll have to stay."

She settled herself cross-legged by the side of the cradle. "Think of a plan!"

Joel and Ben-Muzzy remained unhelpfully silent.

"It's a pity Ben-Muzzy can't turn all the Green Elves invisible," said Gemma.

"That's an idea," said Joel.

"Oh, do you think so?" said Ben-Muzzy. "Well, let me tell you, if I had enough magic to do all that —" He stopped. "I could turn *you* invisible," he said.

"Me?" said Joel and Gemma together.

"One of you," said Ben-Muzzy.

"Me!" said Joel and Gemma.

Ben-Muzzy shook his head. The tip of his hat moved slowly to and fro. "I haven't got enough magic for both of you. I could do one — if you think you wouldn't be scared."

"I wouldn't be scared!" boasted Joel.

"Neither would I!" said Gemma.

"I bet if I were invisible," said Joel, "I could start a panic among those Paddiwack Gnomes!"

"And me, and me!" clamored Gemma. "Do me!"

"He can't do you, he doesn't have enough magic."

"Not if you want to be brought back again. I've told you before," said Ben-Muzzy, "it's not good to stay invisible for too long. I'm taking a big enough risk as it is. I wouldn't be at all surprised if I have great difficulty getting back at all. I'll probably be like a sheet of glass for the next few days. So I'm afraid it's really out of the question."

"Oh, all right, all right," said Gemma. It wasn't at all fair, just because she was a girl. "So what am I supposed to do?"

"You can gather up all the baby elves and take care of them," said Joel kindly.

"Oh, thanks," said Gemma. "Thanks very much."

"Well, someone's got to make themselves responsible," said Joel. "They'll only get trodden on otherwise."

"Humph!" said Gemma. She didn't think it would be nearly so much fun as fighting gnomes. "Well, go on, then!" she said. "Do it! Get it over with! Make him disappear!"

Ben-Muzzy cleared his throat. The tip of his hat moved forward.

"You're sure about this?" said Ben-Muzzy.

"*Yes!*" said the twins together.

"Very well, then. Kindly remain absolutely still and don't fidget, or you'll come out patchy."

The tip of Ben-Muzzy's hat made a half circle through the air, then slowly floated back down. Gemma heard Ben-Muzzy solemnly chanting a spell:

"Wozzible wizzible
Twin invisible.
Boy not girl
From sight unfurl."

Gemma clapped a hand to her mouth as inch
by inch, from the toes upward, her twin began
to vanish.

"Yikes!" said Joel, holding out a fast-disappearing arm.

"You're gone!" squeaked Gemma. "I can't see you anymore!"

"Neither can I," wailed Joel, worried for a minute. "I can't see me anymore!"

"What does it feel like?"

Joel thought about it, trying not to panic.

"Not bad," he said. "I suppose."

I wish he'd done *me,* thought Gemma. Life really was grossly unfair.

Chapter Six

Night had fallen over the Grove of the Green Elves. A small moon hung in the sky, and thousands of stars twinkled and shone. Every bush and every tree was crowded with elves, clinging together in fear of the Paddiwack Gnomes. The soft green light of their eyes lit up the center of the grove, which had been cleared of toadstools to keep them from being trampled underfoot when the fight began.

Gemma was hiding in the middle of a large holly bush with a dozen baby elves. She had unraveled a spider's web and strung it from leaf to leaf, and now each tiny cradle was hanging from it, rocking gently every time Gemma breathed.

Teeno had been sent as a messenger to the Laughing Pixies. When they heard that an invisible wizard and an invisible twin were going to be helping, they had been only too eager to join in. Now they lay in wait on the far side of the stream, hiding in the reeds with stones and pieces of stick, while Joel and Ben-Muzzy (not that anyone could see them) were standing at the entrance to the grove, watching for the first of the enemy to appear.

The hoot of an owl came three times through the night. That was the signal from the Laughing Pixies that the gnomes were on their way, creeping through the forest.

Gemma heard it in her holly bush and picked up a stout club, ready to defend herself and the baby elves should any Paddiwacks discover her hiding place.

Joel and Ben-Muzzy heard it and grasped their handfuls of sharpened twigs, which they were going to use for sticking into unsuspecting gnomes.

The Green Elves heard it in the trees and bushes, and one by one they screwed up their eyes very tightly and the soft green light faded away and the grove was left in the silver glow of the stars.

The first of the Paddiwacks loomed up out of the darkness. They were hard to spot at first, because they had dressed themselves in brown from head to foot and tucked their long yellow beards into their tunics. They came stealing up the path toward the entrance to the grove. Joel and Ben-Muzzy saw them just in time. They jumped on them with wild yells that made even Gemma's blood run cold, and pricked at them with their sharpened twigs.

The gnomes were taken by surprise. They knew the Green Elves never put up any sort of a fight, and they knew the Laughing Pixies had refused to help them anymore, so who could it be, pricking and prodding in the darkness?

Ben-Muzzy jabbed a particularly villainous-looking gnome in the arm. The gnome yelped and jumped backward, bumping into the gnome behind him. Joel was everywhere, slashing and poking, leaping up and down, giving his Indian war cry, batting at every gnome that came anywhere near him.

The gnomes were flung into confusion.

Surrounded on all sides by an enemy they couldn't even see, they began striking out wildly with their pronged sticks. Quite often they hit one another by mistake, and then flew into a panic and began stabbing the air and running blindly into trees. The gnomes at the front blundered back and forth, and the gnomes at the back, not knowing what was happening, made matters worse by trying to press forward.

The fight did not last long. The Paddiwacks, terrified and bewildered, were soon streaming in disarray through the forest.

"Wolla wolla wolla!" caroled Joel, chasing after them.

"Great magic cauldrons!" panted Ben-Muzzy, waving his bunch of sharpened sticks above his head.

He picked up his cloak and raced after Joel. As soon as the Paddiwacks had passed the stream, the Laughing Pixies rose up from their hiding places and began the chase. A huge battle was soon taking place in the forest. The Laughing Pixies, grinning from ear to ear, had far the best of it. The Paddiwacks had not come prepared for a fight, but the Laughing Pixies were having the time of their lives.

As the sounds of battle faded, Gemma left her
holly bush and walked cautiously into the center
of the grove. Suddenly she froze. One gnome,
braver than the rest, had stayed on after the
others had fled. His lips twisted as he came
toward her, holding out his pronged stick.

Gemma held back a scream and stood her ground. Behind her she still held her stout club. As soon as the gnome was near enough, she pulled it out and began to beat him on the shoulders.

"Go away!" she cried. "Go away, you ugly thing! Go back to your stuffy old caves!"

Teeno appeared at her side. Bravely, he leaped at the gnome and bit him on the leg. Gemma hit the gnome on the head with her club. A great cheer went up from the surrounding trees and bushes, and the Green Elves, with a courage thay had never known before, came swarming to the rescue. They darted like quicksilver this way and that, pulling at the gnome's clothes, sinking their teeth into his flesh, prodding him with pine needles, until at last he turned tail and ran.

After that, the Green Elves were very proud and puffed up. The Queen declared that they had won a great victory, and everyone scurried off to gather up the toadstools and lay out a banquet.

"Do stay!" whispered Teeno to Gemma.

"All right," said Gemma. "But I must find Joel

and Ben-Muzzy."

It wasn't easy tracking down an invisible twin and an invisible wizard. The elves were all over the place, twittering and squeaking in their excitement at having fought off the Paddiwacks. Gemma could hardly move without running the risk of crushing one.

"Joel?" she called. "Ben-Muzzy?"

And then she heard it, the curious droning that was Ben-Muzzy saying one of his spells. It sounded at first like bees buzzing. If Gemma hadn't known what it was, she might easily have passed it by.

"*Joel?*" she said, rushing forward.

"Ow!" said Joel's voice.

"Oops!" said Gemma.

"For magic's sake!" snapped Ben-Muzzy.

Gemma picked herself up and rubbed ruefully at her elbow. "Sorry," she said. She giggled. "Didn't see you!"

"No, and if you don't stop blundering into other people's spells," said Joel's voice irritably, "you may never get to see me."

"Sorry, sorry!" Gemma flung up her hands. "I apologize!"

"We must just hope," said Ben-Muzzy, "that nothing has gone wrong. It's an exceedingly dangerous thing to do, interrupting a person in the middle of a spell."

"Sorry, sorry, *sorry,*" whispered Gemma. She put a finger to her lips. "I'll be quiet as a mouse while you do it again."

"Very well, then. Complete stillness, *please*. I will now invoke the powers . . .

> Wozzible wizzible
> Bring us back visible;
> Wizard and twin, from foot to shin,
> And head to knee, for all to see."

"Well!" said Gemma, as the familiar outline of her twin slowly shimmered into view. "Well . . . *yes*."

"Yes what?" said Joel, doing a victory dance in front of her.

"There's a piece of you missing," said Gemma. She tried unsuccessfully not to giggle. "You haven't got any backs to your legs . . . either of you! Only fronts!"

Joel and Ben-Muzzy looked down at themselves, alarmed. What Gemma had said was true. From the knee downward, they didn't have any backs to their legs.

"That's your fault!" shouted Joel. "Interrupting the spell!"

Gemma tossed her head. "Don't you blame me," she said. "It's got nothing to do with me.

He said 'foot to shin.' That's your shin." She pointed. "The front part. Didn't say anything about the back part. Calf's the back part; he left that out."

Ben-Muzzy's face grew slightly pink.

"Is that right?" demanded Joel.

"Ah — hum — well," said Ben-Muzzy. "Yes. Well. In a manner of speaking."

"In that case, you'd jolly well better say another spell *immediately!*" roared Joel. "I can't go to school with half my legs missing!"

By the time Joel and Ben-Muzzy reappeared, covered in scratches but with their legs fully restored, the Queen had forgotten who they were.

"We're having a banquet," she told them, "to celebrate our victory over the Paddiwack Gnomes. I don't know who you are, but as long as you're not goblins, you may join us."

Gemma giggled and handed them each an acorn cup full of dew.

"She's got nerve!" said Joel. "After all we did for her!"

"I'm afraid she's very absentminded," said Teeno.

"I think she must be crazy!" said Ben-Muzzy angrily.

His hands and feet and most of his legs could be seen again, but the middle part of him was still only a vague blur. To think he had stayed invisible simply to help the Green Elves, and now the Queen couldn't even remember who he was!

"I reckon we should be going," decided Joel, handing back his empty acorn cup. "That was a great battle, but it's about time we moved on."

"Oh, do you have to?" said Teeno. "Her Majesty will be most disappointed."

Gemma privately doubted it. She had already heard the Queen ask an elf-in-waiting why goblins had been invited to the party.

"I'm afraid we do," she said. "The Airy Fairies have stolen our broomstick, and we have to try and find it again so that we can get home in time for dinner."

"If it's Airy Fairies," said Teeno, "they'll be up there somewhere, in the clouds. I'll show you how to get there, if you like."

"That would be very kind," said Gemma.

They followed Teeno out of the grove and through the forest, across some marshland where the Will o' the Wisps lived, and into some caves at the foot of a hillside.

"There you are," said Teeno. "Just follow the steps and they'll take you to the top."

"Top of what?" asked Joel.

"Top of the steps," said Teeno.

"But what is *at* the top of the steps?"

Teeno blushed, bright green. "I'm afraid I don't know. I've never been up there. Green Elves don't go adventuring."

"Well, at least it's in the right direction," said Gemma. She always believed in looking on the bright side when you could.

It was a long, steep climb up the steps. Every now and again, they came to wide ledges with the words RESTING PLACE painted on them, where travelers who had gone before had stopped and carved messages.

Beware the Nurdle Bore, read Gemma. Who, she wondered, was the Nurdle Bore?

At last there was a shout from Joel, doggedly plodding ahead: "Sky! I can see sky!"

The sky, when they reached it, was bright cornflower blue, full of fat white clouds hurriedly scooting along in the breeze. They scanned it eagerly, but not a sign was there of the Airy Fairies.

"*Now* what do we do?" said Gemma.

"And where *are* we?" added Joel.

Ben-Muzzy shook his head. He sank dejectedly onto the grass. The Airy Fairies could be anywhere. What chance did he stand of ever catching up with them? Even if his magic had come back, which it might be starting to do, how could you say a spell for going somewhere when you had no idea where it was you wanted to go?

"I can tell you where we are," said Gemma, "if that's any help. We're in the land of the Great Nurdle Bore . . . whoever he is."

"What?" Ben-Muzzy's head came up so fast that his hat nearly fell off. "How do you know?"

"'Cause it says so," said Gemma simply. She nodded at a signpost which the others, in their anxious scanning of the sky, had missed. The signpost had one arm, pointing straight ahead. On the arm were the words, **To the land of the Great Nurdle Bore**.

"We could be in luck!" cried Ben-Muzzy. Suddenly energetic, he leapt to his feet. "If there's one person who can tell us where the broomstick is, it's the Great Nurdle Bore!"

"How would he know?" said Joel.

"He'd know," said Ben-Muzzy. "He knows everything, the Nurdle Bore."

Gemma giggled frivolously. "I hope he's not

as boring as he sounds!"

"He is," said Ben-Muzzy. "He's the most boring person in the whole universe. It's because of knowing everything. It makes him incredibly and excruciatingly boring. People fall asleep in droves just listening to him."

"And you're telling us," said Joel, "that we've got to go and see this incredibly and excruciatingly boring person?"

"Yes," said Ben-Muzzy. "It's the only way to get the broomstick back."

"Then let's go," said Joel.

Ben-Muzzy hesitated. He seemed on the verge of saying something, then changed his mind.

"All right." He turned to Gemma. "Look at me very carefully," he said. "Am I visible again?"

Gemma looked. "Yes!" she said. "All over!"

"Then let's find three oak trees and get going."

"Oak trees!" Gemma clapped her hands. Oak trees could mean only one thing: Ben-Muzzy's magic had come back! Oak trees were what he used for very special, powerful spells — spells for coming-and-going.

"Hurrah!" cried Gemma. "We're off!"

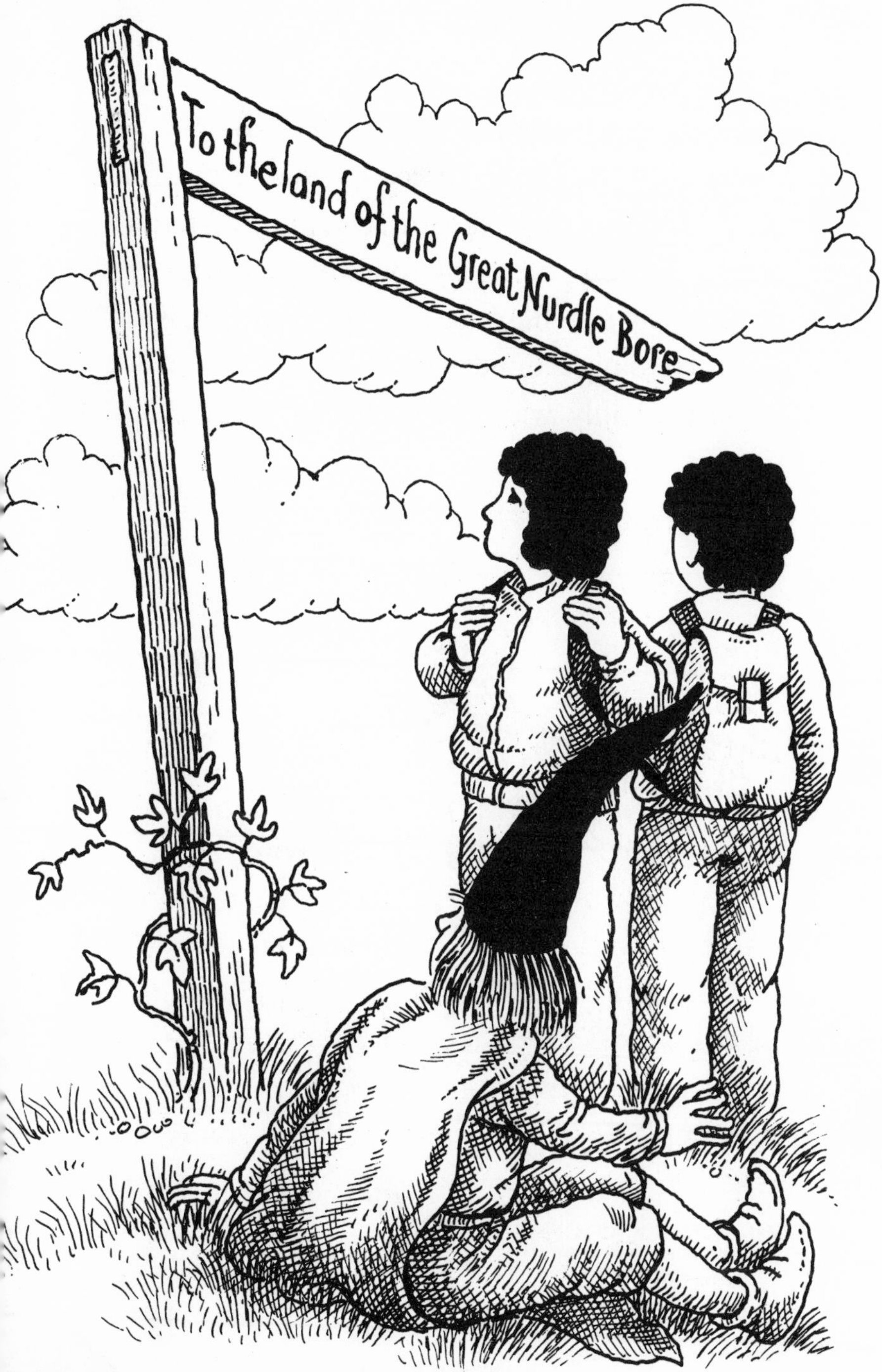
To the land of the Great Nurdle Bore

"Hang on! Hang on!" Joel wasn't going to be rushed. He may have agreed to go and visit the most boring man in the universe, but he hadn't agreed to get there by one of Ben-Muzzy's notoriously unreliable spells. "What do we want to go messing around with magic for when we could probably walk there in five minutes?"

"Because we're tired," said Gemma. "And we're in a hurry. Imagine being scared," she said scornfully, "of a little bit of magic!"

"It's perfectly safe," said Ben-Muzzy. "I know what I'm doing. Form a magic circle and let's get moving!"

Obediently, within the shelter of three oak trees, the twins linked hands with Ben-Muzzy.

"OK," said Ben-Muzzy. "Close your eyes and around we go . . . off to the land of the Great Nurdle Bore!"

Chapter Seven

There was a flash of blue light and the magic circle rose into the air, turned twice in a westerly direction, and disappeared.

Gemma, still clutching Joel and Ben-Muzzy's hands, felt as if she were being sucked up by a great vacuum cleaner. Before she had time to feel properly apprehensive (because it had to be said, Ben-Muzzy's spells were *not* always reliable), the vacuum cleaner had blown them out again — *pflup!* — like corks popping out of a bottle.

Gemma looked around. They were standing on what seemed to be an old-fashioned village green, with a drinking fountain and a war memorial and a duck pond, on which floated three bright-red ducks with orange beaks that looked like dinner plates.

"*Well?*" said Joel. "Are we or aren't we?"

Ben-Muzzy twitched grandly at his cloak. "Of course we are!" Hadn't he told them? He knew what he was doing! (All the same, it came as a relief to Ben-Muzzy, too. You could never be *totally* sure about spells for coming-and-going. They sometimes took you to some very odd places.)

"OK, so where's this old nurdling Bore hang out, then?" demanded Joel.

"He lives in an ivory tower," said Ben-Muzzy, "at the top of a high hill."

Joel looked around. "Well, there's a high hill," he said. He put a hand over his eyes to shade them from the sun. "And there's some kind of tower at the top of it."

"If we're going to climb all that way," said Gemma, "I need a drink."

She walked over to the fountain and pressed the plunger. Instantly a spray of rainbow-colored water shot out.

"*Oh!*" gasped Gemma.

Joel studied her, interested. "Did you know

you've turned all colors of the rainbow? Your nose has a huge purple stripe down it."

Gemma screeched.

"That will teach you to go touching things," said Joel.

He wandered over to the war memorial and studied the list of names. *"In memory of those who went up the High Hill and did not return....* What d'you suppose that means?"

"Ah — hm . . . yes," said Ben-Muzzy. "Yes. Well — yes."

There was a silence. Gemma scrubbed her purple nose.

"Yes *what?*" said Joel.

"Yes. Well —" Ben-Muzzy cleared his throat. "The fact is — I — ah — I forgot to mention —"

Joel looked at him sternly. "What did you forget to mention?"

"I forgot to mention," gabbled Ben-Muzzy, "that it is *rumored* — only *rumored,* mind you — that the Great Nurdle Bore is capable of boring people stiff."

"Oh! Is that all?" Joel relaxed. "We've got a teacher at school who does that. Mr. Breary. We call him Dreary. He's so boring, people fall asleep and snore."

"I'm not talking about people falling asleep and snoring. I'm talking about people being bored stiff. I'm not worried for myself, of course. *I'll* be all right," said Ben-Muzzy. "I'm a wizard."

"And *I'll* be all right," said Joel, "'cause I'm used to Dreary."

They both turned to consider Gemma, busy spitting on her handkerchief and scraping her nose.

"Maybe just we two should go," said Joel.

"What?" Gemma's head shot up. "You're not leaving me behind!"

"But it could be dangerous," said Ben-Muzzy.

"You could get bored stiff," said Joel. "It's all right for me. I'm used to it, with Dreary."

"What d'you think I am?" said Gemma.

"You probably don't get bored as easily as I do. Girls don't," said Joel.

"Oh, don't they? In that case, you ought to be the one to stay. If you're so easily bored, you'll be bored stiff in no time."

"Not me!" boasted Joel. "I'll simply shut my ears and stop listening."

"If we don't listen," said Gemma, "there really won't be much point in going to see him. *Will* there?"

Gemma smiled sweetly with rainbow-colored lips. Joel scowled.

"What exactly are we going to ask him, anyway?" he said.

"Where the broomstick is, I would *think*," said Gemma.

"No, no, no!" Ben-Muzzy was shocked.

(Ha! thought Joel. Gemma needn't think she knew everything, because she obviously didn't.)

"You never ask him a question straight out. He has to arrive at things," said Ben-Muzzy, "in what might be called a roundabout fashion. It's what comes of being an expert. He can't give a straight answer to a straight question. He has too much knowledge for that."

"So, what will you say?" asked Gemma as they set off up the High Hill.

"I'll say, 'Which way does the wind blow, Sir?'" replied Ben-Muzzy.

"And how will that tell us what we want to know?"

"It will tell us which direction to go, to begin with. And if we listen carefully enough, it will tell us — in a roundabout fashion — where the broomstick is."

"I'll listen carefully," volunteered Gemma.

"You?" Joel couldn't resist a little scoffing.

"You couldn't listen carefully if your life depended on it!"

"Besides," cautioned Ben-Muzzy, as Gemma indignantly opened her mouth, "listening carefully is the very thing that's dangerous. The more carefully you listen, the more likely you are to get bored."

Joel nodded. "Like with Dreary. We'll do the listening. You just sit and daydream."

It was as long and steep a climb up the High Hill as it had been through the caves. They met no one at all coming down, but halfway up they overtook an old woman herding ants. Gemma, always polite, said, "Good afternoon! What beautiful ants."

The old woman stopped herding and leaned on her stick. "And where be you a-going, my ducky?"

"We're off to see the Great Nurdle Bore," said Gemma.

"You must be desperate folk if that's your goal."

"There's a question we have to ask him, you see. He's the only person in the whole world who can help."

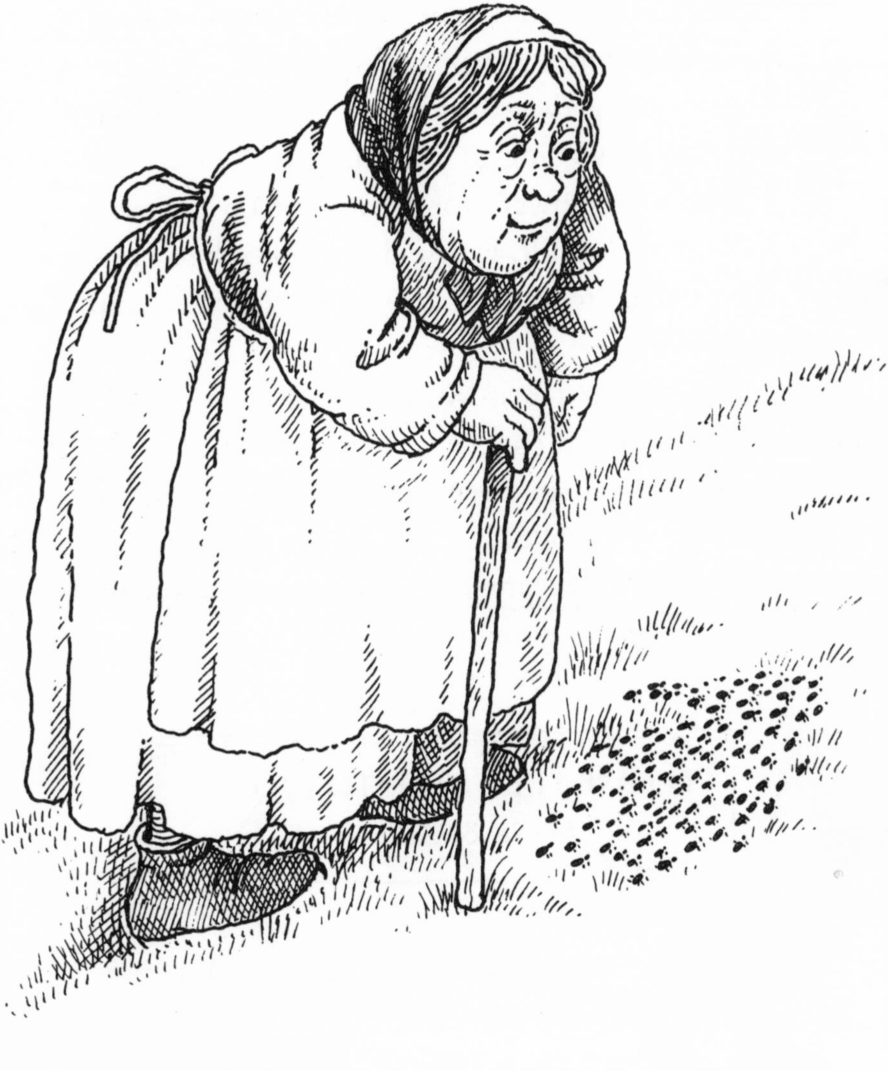

"Well, if that be the case —" the old woman skillfully rounded up a couple of ants which had strayed from the main herd —"I'll bid you good-bye right here and now. There's few as have returned from a journey up the hill."

"*I'm* going to return," said Joel. "No stupid old Nurdle's going to bore me stiff!"

The ivory tower stood by itself on the very summit of the hill. It rose dizzily into the air, its top seeming to sway as they tilted their heads to look at it.

"Right," said Ben-Muzzy.

"Right," said Joel.

Ben-Muzzy smacked a hand onto the top of his hat. Joel rolled up the sleeves of his track suit. Gemma, meanwhile, had found a door. By the side of the door was a notice that said:

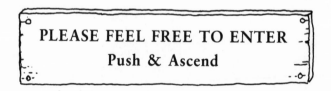

PLEASE FEEL FREE TO ENTER
Push & Ascend

Gemma pushed. The door swung open.
"Here we are!" said Gemma.

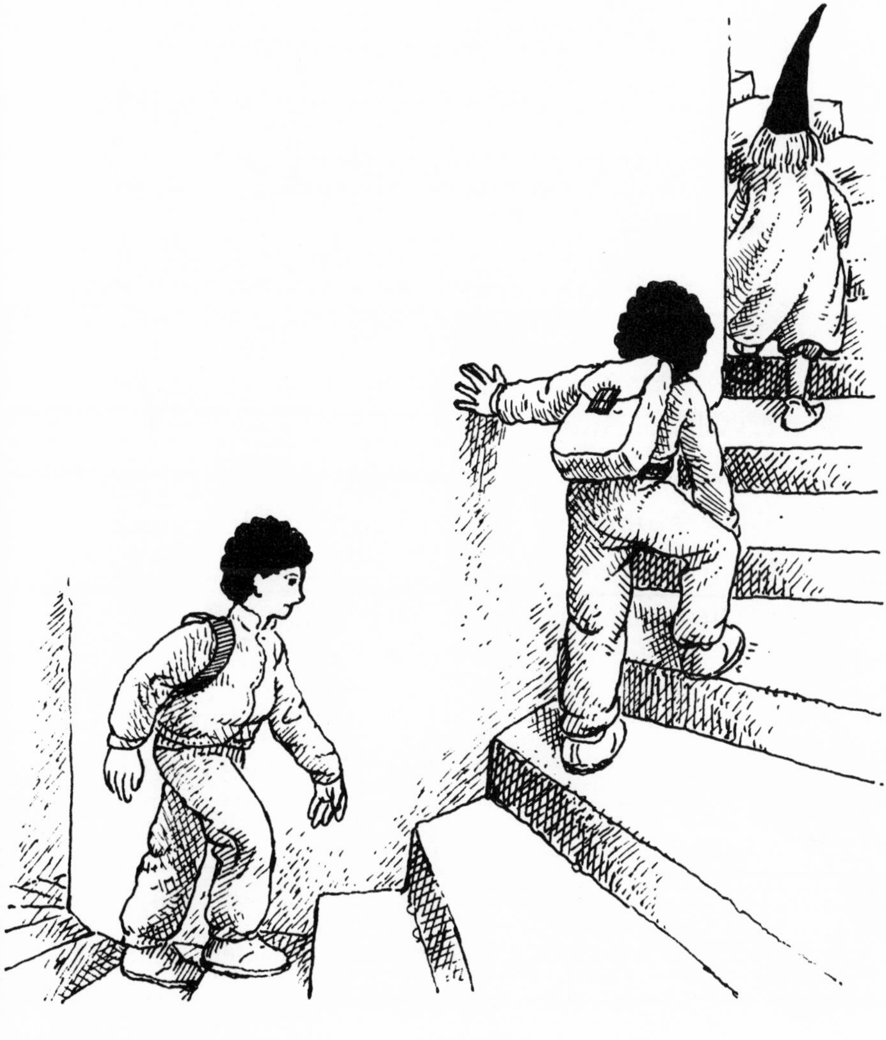

"More steps," groaned Ben-Muzzy.

The steps in the tower went around and around. Around and around, and up and up. Step after step after step after step. Gemma lost count after the first five hundred.

One hour later they reached the top of the tower.

They came upon it suddenly, around a bend. They knew it was the top because there weren't any more steps. Instead, there was a circular room full from floor to ceiling with books. Books in piles, books in heaps. Books everywhere. And through the middle of them, a narrow passage.

After a moment's hesitation, Ben-Muzzy led the way. (He would rather not have led the way, but he *was* the one who had lost the broomstick.)

The passage wound through a maze of dusty volumes. Some were so old, they had turned yellow at the edges, others were riddled with bookworms. After several twists and turns, the passage ended in a musty cocoon, in the center of which, hunched over an old wooden desk covered with quill pens and ink pots, sat the

Great Nurdle Bore.

As the twins and Ben-Muzzy entered, he pushed back his chair and rose to his feet . . . rose and rose and went on rising. He was the longest, thinnest person that Gemma had ever seen.

He was pale as fungus, like a damp gray toadstool growing in a bog. His lank black hair was parted in the middle, straggling down on either side of his face with its wet lipless mouth and deep-sunk eyes that were like pools of black slime. From his pendulous nose the boogers hung, glistening in and out as he breathed.

(Too busy reading books, Gemma supposed, to use his handkerchief.) He was wearing a long black coat and big black boots on his long, splayed feet. His fingers waved like damp tentacles, leaving blotches on everything they touched.

"How charming! I see I have company," he said.

He spat as he spoke, his lipless mouth wriggling and writhing like a thin pink worm.

"Two sweet children and a wizard, if I am not mistaken. And what, my dear ones, can I do for you? Pray make yourselves at home! Take a seat! No need to stand on ceremony."

Gemma, after casting around in vain for a chair, nervously seated herself on a pile of books. Joel and Ben-Muzzy rather sternly remained standing.

"Mmm?" crooned the Bore, fixing Gemma with his slippy, slimy gaze.

Gemma sat up straight on her pile of books. "We wanted to ask you," she said, "if it's not putting you to too much trouble — that is, if you don't think we're being too much of a nuisance —"

"What we would like to know," said Ben-

Muzzy, coming to her aid, "is which way the wind blows. Sir," he added, remembering his manners.

"Ah!" The Bore spread his tentacles. (Gemma recoiled as one drifted unpleasantly near her.) "Who has seen the wind? Neither you nor I —"

"Yes, well, that's true," said Gemma. "I'm very sorry we troubled you and I think maybe we should be going."

Something inside her said they should never have come. She half-rose from her pile of books, but before she could get to her feet, the Bore had started up again.

"Wind that blows through me, wind that follows fast, warm wind, wet wind, west wind, wanton wind, winds that will be howling, winds will call the darkness, winds of the world, winds of the west, wind —"

— of the western sea, thought Gemma. They had sung a song at school about the wind of the western sea. How had it gone? *Sweet and low, sweet and low, wind of the western sea! Blow, blow, breeze and blow* —

She had just reached the line "Sleep, my little one," when she realized to her horror that her eyes were glazing over. She jerked herself awake to hear the Bore's voice still nurdling on. "Wind and his nobility, wind and the rain, wind blows and leaves are scattered, wind is chill, wind shall blow for ever more, wind —"

Gemma began to think that she would have been better off staying on her feet with Joel and Ben-Muzzy. Sitting on the books was too comfortable. She tried to stand up, but her limbs seemed to have turned to stone. Slowly and with difficulty, she turned her head toward Ben-Muzzy. Why wasn't he saying anything? They had come here to find which way the wind was blowing, not to sit through all these boring bits of poetry, if that's what they were.

". . . wind blow, wind —"

"Blows where?" croaked Gemma. "Wind blows where?"

"Wind bloweth where it listeth, wind bloweth a gale. . . . This is the shipping forecast. There are warnings of gales in Fogarty, Biscuit, Peabody, Grundy, Doggerel, Fishnet, and Shallow. The area forecast. Viking southeasterly 3 or 4, increasing 5 or 6 —"

Why didn't Ben-Muzzy say something?

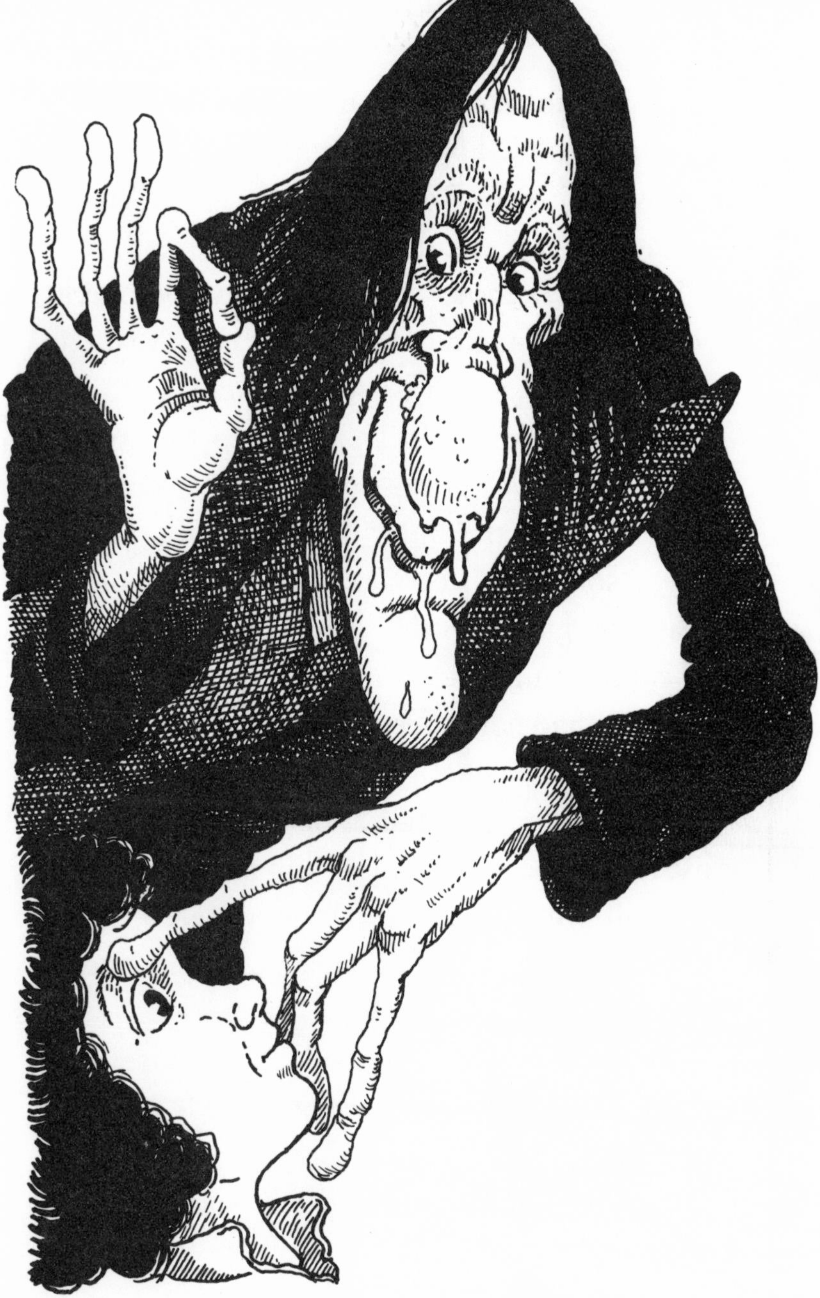

"— occasional rain, moderate or poor, becoming good. Fogarty, southeasterly 3 or 4, increasing 5 or 6. Rain later —"

A huge yawn engulfed Gemma.

"Biscuit, Peabody, southeasterly becoming cyclonic, 3 or 4. Rain or showers. Moderate or good. Grundy, south or southeasterly —"

Zzzzzzz, went Joel and Ben-Muzzy in chorus.

Drone, went the Bore.

". . . southeast veering southwest, 5 or 6, occasional gale 8. Rain, then showers —"

Gemma struggled against an onrushing tide of sleep. She had never been so bored in all her life!

"Doggerel, Fishnet, Shallow —"

Concentrate, thought Gemma. I'm supposed — to be — l-i-s-t-e-n-iiiiiiiiiiiiing.

"— all winds reaching Deep Sea area 1600, dropping sharply, expected calm. General outlook —"

Gemma's eyelids drooped. She must stay awake. *She had to stay awake.* Iggledy obbledy uggledy in . . .

"— and that is the end of the shipping forecast for inshore waters. Waters rolling from their mountain springs. World of waters dark and deep. Water, water, everywhere. Waters quiet as the shore. Quiet, quiet. Are you all asleep, my dear ones?"

A tentacle snaked out and pried open one of Gemma's eyelids. Gemma saw the palsied white mushroom face of the Bore almost on top of her. She smelled the hot, stale smell of his bad eggy breath. She tried to open her mouth to scream, but her lips refused to move. She tried to jump up and run, but not a muscle stirred. Gemma was as stiff as a board.

Happily, the Bore hummed a tuneless dirge to himself as he inspected his victims. Three more for his collection!

"Down we go, my treasures . . ."

There was a grinding sound as the Bore pulled a lever. The piece of floor on which Gemma was sitting, on which Joel and Ben-Muzzy stood stiffly side by side, began slowly to descend into the black depths of the tower.

Chapter Eight

The chunk of floor plummeted downward through the darkness. There was no danger of anyone falling off: Gemma, Ben-Muzzy, and Joel were all as stiff as boards. Only in one small corner of Gemma's brain was there still a faint flicker of life.

"Deep Sea," it kept saying. "Deep Sea."

It was really irritating, especially as she didn't know what it meant.

The floor juddered to a halt, somewhere down in the dark. There was a long silence, then the sound of a door creaking on its hinges, and a light appeared. Behind the light was the Great Nurdle Bore.

Still happily humming his dirge, the Bore set

the light on a shelf and pressed a switch by the side of the door. Gemma felt herself being slid forward, along with Joel and Ben-Muzzy and the books she was sitting on.

"Now, let me see . . . let me see." The Bore rubbed his tentacles together. "Where shall we put you, my dears? We shall have to find you somewhere special. It's not every day one has the pleasure of entertaining a wizard and a pair of twins . . . I think perhaps over here —"

The Bore pressed again at his switch and the twins and Ben-Muzzy swiveled in a half circle and shot like wind-up toys across the floor.

"Or how about here? Or maybe here . . .? Yes! I think here will do very nicely. Next to my most important guest . . . this is one of the daughters of the Queen of the Shallow Isles. She's been with me for almost ten years. And how are you today, my dear? Your Highness, I should say. The Princess Chlora . . . always such an honor to entertain royalty. There we are, then, my treasures."

The Bore picked up his light, pressed the switch again and stepped onto the chunk of floor.

"You get yourselves settled in," he said, "and I'll be down to talk to you later. Until then, my darlings —" The Bore kissed his tentacles to them as the floor began its long journey back up the tower. "I'll leave you the light, so you can get to know one another. See you soon."

Silence fell. Not a sound could be heard, down in the cold dark depths. Not a voice spoke, not a limb moved.

Gemma's eyelids kept trying to close. They felt as though they had lead weights attached to them. Painfully, she forced them to stay open. She was still sitting on her pile of books, but by swiveling her eyes to the left she could make out a pair of feet which she was almost certain were Ben-Muzzy's — she could just see the red, curly tips of his slippers. To the right was another pair, clad in silver sandals. The Princess Chlora?

Across the room, still at floor level, were more feet. Feet in boots, feet in shoes, bare feet, black feet, brown feet, white feet. Gemma couldn't lift her head to see higher than the ankles, her neck was too stiff. But at least she was managing to keep her eyes open. If she concentrated really hard, she might be able to unstiffen the rest of herself before the Bore came back and started lecturing them.

"Deep Sea, Deep Sea," muttered the voice in the corner of Gemma's brain.

Never mind the Deep Sea, she thought. We've got to get out of here!

Little by little, as the effects of the Bore began to wear off, Gemma's limbs came back to life. The first thing she was able to move was her head. She turned it to the left and saw Ben-Muzzy and her twin, standing rigidly at attention, eyes closed, arms by their sides. She turned it to the right and saw the Princess Chlora, who had been there for ten years. The Princess Chlora, in her silver sandals and brocade gown, with a tiara tipped rakishly over one eye, was sitting bolt upright in a chair. Her cheeks were pink and waxy, her lips cherry red. She looked like a doll in a toy-shop window.

All around the room, stacked by the dozens on shelves and tables, some arranged in groups, some sitting, some standing, some on pedestals, were the living sculptures of the people who had climbed the High Hill and never returned.

The ones on the lower shelves were brightly

polished and free of dust, but most of the ones higher up were covered in grime and cobwebs. They must have been there the longest; or possibly the Nurdle Bore grew bored with some of the people he had bored, and simply bundled them out of the way and forgot them.

Gemma shivered. With a determined effort, she wobbled to her feet, stepped stiffly down from the shelf, and shuffled along the floor on cardboardy legs until she was directly in front of Joel and Ben-Muzzy.

"Joel!" she said. "Ben-Muzzy!" She tried shaking them, she tried prying their eyelids apart, she tried shouting in their ears, but Joel and Ben-Muzzy had joined the ranks of the living dead. There seemed no way of ever waking them.

But there had to be! She had come back —
why hadn't they?

Maybe, she thought, it was like going to the
dentist. You had to wait for the injection to
wear off, and with her it had worn off quicker
than it had with the others. If the Bore would
only stay away long enough, or could be
stopped from talking . . . it was the talking
that did it. There must be *some* way you
could keep a person from talking.

Gemma sank down onto the edge of the shelf, next to the princess. As she did so, she felt something soft and squidgy in the pocket of her track suit. She put her hand in. Ugh! Yucky toffee! Distastefully, holding the edge of the packet between finger and thumb, she pulled it out. *Stickjaw Toffee! Guaranteed to stick jaws.* Joel had meant to give it to Graham Roberts, to keep him from talking in class. It wouldn't be much use now.

Or would it?

Suddenly Gemma had an idea.

She had it not a moment too soon. Hardly had it come to her before she heard the creaking of hinges. The Bore had come back to bore them! He was talking even as he came through the door. He probably had been talking all the way down from his ivory tower. He probably never *stopped* talking.

". . . lecture on the Merdish Qualities of the Downbend Factor in Grotal Analysis. Are you all sitting comfortably, my pretties? All right, then, I'll begin. Grotal analysis, in its merdish aspect —"

"I don't want to hear about grotal analysis in

its merdish aspect!" Gemma sprang to her feet, confronting the Bore. "I don't want to hear about it in *any* aspect!"

The Bore blinked. "You don't?" he said.

"No, I don't!" said Gemma. "I don't know what it is, but whatever it is, it sounds dead boring and I don't want to hear!"

"I see." The Bore stroked his chin with a bunch of tentacles. He seemed taken aback. "I shall have to think about this," he said.

"Well, while you're thinking," said Gemma, "why not have a piece of toffee?"

"Toffee. Sugar Plum. Candy. Caramel. Chocolate. Marzipan. Lollipop. Butterscotch. Liquorice. Marshmallow. Chewing Gum. Gobstopper. Peppermint. Bull's Eye. Fudge. T——"

Gemma felt her eyes begin to glaze. "*Have* some!" she said.

"Thank you. I will." The Bore ripped off a great gooey chunk and stuffed it into his mouth. "Turkish Delight. Gummy Bears. Jelly Babies. Sher——"

He stopped.

"Sherbet Lemons?" said Gemma.

The Bore made a strangulated sound. His lipless mouth worked frantically as his eyes rolled in their sockets. His tentacles came up and tried in vain to tear his jaws apart. They wouldn't move. They were stuck fast! With a muted scream of horror, the Bore turned and fled the room.

"Quick!" Gemma rushed at Joel and Ben-Muzzy. "Wake up! *Joel . . . WAKE UP!*"

Slowly, one of Joel's eyelids fluttered open. He stared unseeing at his twin.

"?" said Joel.

"It's me!" cried Gemma.

Joel swallowed. Next to him, Ben-Muzzy's voice moaned, "Where am I?"

Gemma spun around. "You're down in the dungeons of the Great Nurdle Bore. We've got to get out! Fast!"

"Can't move," groaned Ben-Muzzy.

"Nonsense! Of course you can! Come on, now!" scolded Gemma, sounding uncommonly like their gym teacher at school. "Make an effort! Take a deep breath!"

"Can't," gasped Joel.

"No such word as can't! Get those limbs

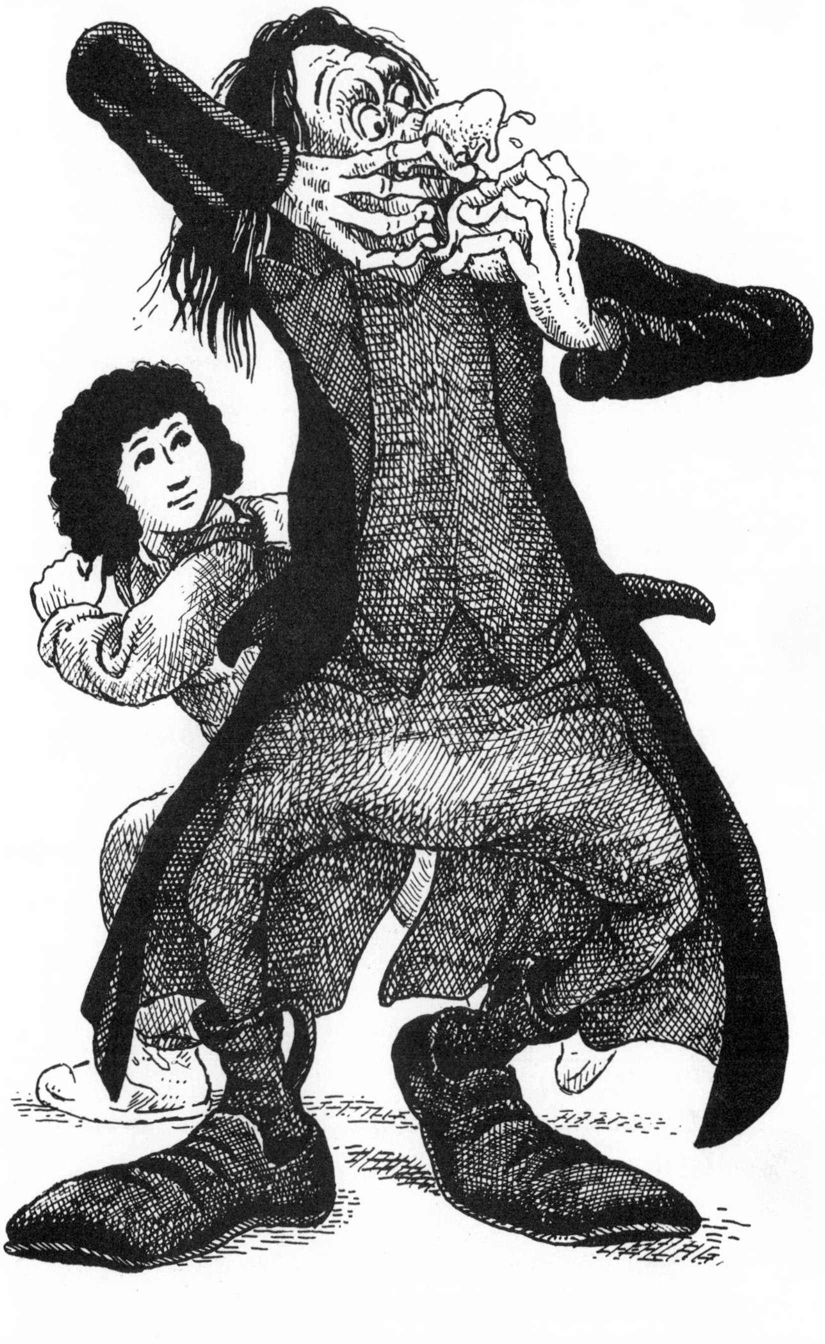

moving, before he comes back and starts boring everyone again!" He wouldn't fall for the toffee trick a second time. If they didn't get out now, they never would. They would be left to molder here forever. "Just do what I tell you!" screamed Gemma.

Ben-Muzzy breathed in, a long shuddering breath. Joel lurched forward on one leg.

"Good!" said Gemma. "Now —"

Too late — already she could hear the creaking of the hinges.

In panic, Gemma flew across the room, hurling herself at the door and slamming it shut. There was a howl of pain from the other side. Serves him right, thought Gemma. Hurriedly, she turned the key in the lock and shot the big iron bolts both top and bottom.

"Treasure, let me in," whimpered the Bore. "I want to talk to you!"

"You mean you want to bore us," said Gemma.

"I want to tell you things! I want to chat with you! I want to hold a conversation! I want to gossip! I want to orate! I w——"

"You go away!" shouted Gemma. "We've

been talked at enough!"

All around her, the living dead were slowly returning to life. After all those years of being bored stiff they were naturally a little confused. People on the upper shelves were distractedly picking the cobwebs from their hair, people on the lower shelves warily testing their legs. The Princess Chlora was setting her tiara to rights.

"So, how do we get out?" said Joel. "Now that you've gone and bolted us in?"

"I know! Everyone do what I'm doing . . . look!" Gemma danced into the center of the room, her fingers stuffed deep into her ears. Obediently, all the people on the shelves clambered down to join her. They, too, stuffed their fingers deep into their ears.

"Whatever you do," yelled Gemma, *"don't take them out!* I'm going to open the door now . . . everybody ready?"

All of the people solemnly nodded. Gemma removed one finger, slid back the bolt, and turned the key. Instantly the Great Nurdle Bore was in with them, slinking through the door, talking as he came.

"Oh, my treasures, my dear ones, my darlings —"

Quickly, Gemma stuffed her fingers back.

"Sorry!" she called. "Can't stop!"

Up the stairs raced Gemma, followed by Joel, by Ben-Muzzy, by the Princess, by all the people who had come back to life and scrambled down from the shelves. The Great Nurdle Bore ran after them, imploring, tears in his eyes, waving

his tentacles. No one took any notice because no one could hear.

Out through the front door poured Gemma and her band. Down the High Hill they streamed, some laughing, some crying, some shouting aloud for sheer joy. A few, more nervous than the rest, still had their fingers rammed in their ears, though they were safe now, for the Great Nurdle Bore never left his ivory tower.

"What happened?" panted Ben-Muzzy as they reached the village green at the foot of the hill. "How did we end up in that dungeon place?"

"He bored you there," said Gemma. "Both of you . . . you both got bored stiff!"

"*I* did?" Ben-Muzzy's jaw fell open. "But I'm a wizard!"

"Yes," said Gemma. "And he's a boy." She jerked her thumb at Joel. "It didn't seem to do you very much good, did it?"

Ben-Muzzy fiddled with his cloak. He looked abashed. Joel, defiant, tossed his head.

"I told you," he said. "I said girls didn't get bored as easily as boys. And it was totally pointless anyway, as far as I can see. We still don't know where the broomstick is!"

Chapter Nine

Ben-Muzzy sank into a heap at the foot of the water fountain. Joel was right. They still didn't know where the broomstick was.

Two big tears rolled off the end of Ben-Muzzy's nose and went sploshing onto the grass. How was he going to go back and face Wollibar without the broomstick? He wouldn't be allowed to say spells or stir the magic cauldron ever again.

"O-o-o-o-o-h!" wailed Ben-Muzzy.

Gemma hadn't the heart to remind him that losing the broomstick was entirely his own fault. Not even Joel was unkind enough to point out that he shouldn't have taken it in the first place. The twins stood awkwardly watching as Ben-

Muzzy wept into a corner of his handkerchief.

"There's got to be *some* way," Joel said. "How far do Airy Fairies travel?"

"As far as the wind blows," wept Ben-Muzzy. "And the wind could b-blow anyw-where!"

In a little dark hole at the back of Gemma's brain, something was stirring.

"Don't they have weather forecasts?" said Joel. "Like on television? Don't they —"

Gemma's voice cut across him: "All winds reaching Deep Sea area 1600," chanted Gemma. "Dropping sharply, expected calm."

There was a pause.

"I beg your pardon?" said Joel.

"All winds reaching Deep Sea area 1600," chanted Gemma. "Dropping sharply, expected calm."

"What's that supposed to mean?"

"All winds reaching —"

"Yes, yes, yes!" said Joel. "You've said that once — you've said it twice! What's it *mean*?"

Gemma shook herself. "I don't know," she said. What did it mean? Suddenly, she remembered. "It's a weather forecast! It's what the Bore said . . . winds reaching Deep Sea area

1600! What's the time?"

Joel looked at his watch. "Five to four."

"And what's 1600?"

"Four o'clock," said Joel, doing a quick calculation on his fingers.

"That means we've got five minutes!" Gemma turned eagerly to Ben-Muzzy. "Can we get to the Deep Sea in five minutes?"

"Don't know what good it'll do, even if we can." Ben-Muzzy blotted despondently at his eyes. "If the broomstick's going to be dropped right in the middle of it —"

"It's got to be worth a try!"

"Yes, it has," said Joel, feeling the time had come for him to assert himself. Gemma had been a little too bossy back there in the dungeon. "Get up and dry your eyes and let's form a circle."

Ben-Muzzy sniffed. He wiped his nose across the back of his hand. "I don't know if I've got enough magic left."

"Of course you have!" said Joel. "Come on, or we'll be too late! There're some oak trees over there. Let's get on with it."

They found three oak trees growing close

together, formed a circle inside them, joined hands, and waited for a still-tearful Ben-Muzzy to start his spell.

"Quick!" said Gemma.

"It's no use hurrying me," said Ben-Muzzy. "These things can't be rushed. I have to make sure that my hat is straight. Wizards can't do spells if their hats are on crooked."

"It's not on crooked."

"It feels crooked."

"Well, it's not!"

"The time," said Joel, in an expressionless voice like a talking clock, "is now two minutes to four precisely."

"Oh, all right. But don't blame me if I run out of magic halfway through . . . wizards aren't made of magic, you know."

Ben-Muzzy held out his hands and screwed his eyes tightly shut. The spell began.

"Fillivan fullivan
Upwigo —"

Ben-Muzzy's hat sailed majestically into the air.

"From this place we wish to go
Somewhere else, more fast than slow.
Pray take us now, the twins and me
To the shore of the Deep Sea."

The wind caught them and whirled them up;
the wind carried them and set them down.

Gemma opened her eyes.

"Sand!" cried Gemma.

"You've done it!" cried Joel.

"You really are getting *very* good at this," they
told Ben-Muzzy.

Ben-Muzzy attempted a smile, but his top lip
puckered and his lower lip quivered. There was
the Deep Sea all right — but where was the
broomstick?

"I can see the Airy Fairies!" yelled Joel.
"There, along the beach!"

Joel took off in a triumphant gallop. A group
of Airy Fairies were darting around over the
rocks, skimming the surface of the rock pools,
squealing and squeaking among themselves. As
Joel thundered up they scattered, twittering,
into the air. Joel shook his fist.

"Where's our broomstick?" he shouted.

"What have you done with our broomstick?"

By way of reply, the Airy Fairies only tittered behind their hands in an irritating fashion. One or two stuck out their tongues. Some even made rude noises.

Stupid creatures! thought Joel.

Between them, he and Gemma began to search the shore (Ben-Muzzy was too sunk in gloom to do more than sit on a breakwater and watch), but the broomstick was nowhere to be found.

"It must have gone out to sea," sighed Gemma. "I suppose we can't p——"

She broke off as something landed with a loud *whumpf!* beside her. Hot breath blew down her neck.

"Hilloo!" said a walloper.

"Oh," said Gemma. "It's you."

"Is it?" said the walloper. He looked around him in surprise. "So it is! Does I know you?"

"You might," said Gemma. "But then again, you might not."

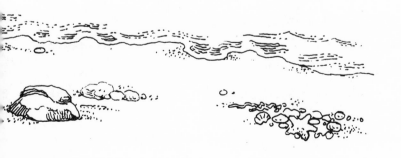

"Never mind," said the walloper. "Want some grub?"

"No, thank you." Gemma shook her head. "I'm not really hungry."

"I is," said the walloper. "I'se going to have grub."

"Don't you ever think about anything else?" said Gemma. "Anything except grub?"

"Yush," said the walloper.

"What? For instance?"

"More grub." The walloper chortled happily. He opened his pouch and began rummaging inside it. "Let's see what we is having here . . . don't want that! Don't want this! Don't want that! Don't want —"

"Hang on!" cried Gemma, ducking as an assortment of twigs and branches began to sail past her ears. "What's that you've got?"

"This? Just some old broomstick wot I find. Don't want that!" The broomstick also went sailing past Gemma's ears. Straight out to sea, it sailed.

"Oh! Quick! Someone rescue it!" wailed Gemma.

Ben-Muzzy, helpless, flapped on the

breakwater. How could he rescue it? Wizards couldn't swim! It was Joel who came charging back down the beach, bravely dived in, right up to his neck, and forged back to shore with the broomstick safely clasped in one hand.

"Oh, terrific!" said Gemma. "Truly terrific! I knew things would work out!" She beamed happily. "Now we can go back to Wonderland!"

"No we c-*can't*," said Joel. "I'm s-soaking wet and f-freezing cold and we've got to g-get home in t-time for dinner."

"Yes, and I should be getting back," said Ben-Muzzy, tenderly wiping the broomstick on his cloak, "before Wollibar discovers."

"Or before you g-go and l-lose the thing again!"

Ben-Muzzy blushed. "Next time I'll take more care."

"Next time you'd better ask Wollibar first," said Joel.

The journey back was far less bumpy than the journey out. Ben-Muzzy wasn't so cocky now. He flew more carefully. Joel, on the other hand, after his daring rescue of the broomstick, was feeling very pleased with himself.

"A little more practice," he said kindly, as they made a perfect landing in the middle of Three Penny Wood, "and you might almost be ready to pass your test."

"Don't take any notice of him," said Gemma.

She leaned forward to whisper in Ben-Muzzy's ear. "I think your spells are getting really good!"

Sick, thought Joel. She was *kissing* him.

"Come again soon," said Gemma.

"Maybe on All Spells Day," said Ben-Muzzy. His eyes gleamed. "We play all sorts of tricks on All Spells Day. I might come and surprise you, dressed as a witch!"

"*That* would be fun," said Gemma.

"Have a good trip back," said Joel, thinking of his dinner.

"And take care," begged Gemma.

Ben-Muzzy, confidence restored, stepped airily astride the broomstick.

"Getting back is elementary," he said. He wafted a hand. "*Emoh em ekat!*"

As the twins stood waving, the broomstick rose steadily from the ground, circled once, dipped in salute, and then was gone.

"Showing off," said Joel. "And that reminds me, have you still got my toffee?"

"No, I don't," said Gemma. "I gave it to the Bore."

"Gave it to the Bore? Gave my toffee to the Bore?"

"Well, I had to do *some*thing," said Gemma, "to keep him from talking. You weren't doing very much, just standing there all stiff and stupid."

"Pooh!" said Joel. "And I don't know what Mom's going to say," he added. "You've still got that purple stripe down your nose . . ."